Lady Justice and the Vigilante gets double thumbs up!

The 7th novel in the Walt Williams Mystery Comedy series is well written with a tight plot, complete with several sub-plots that keep you wondering how author Robert Thornhill is going to bring the tale to a satisfactory conclusion.

It also provides an opportunity to ponder the ethics of vigilantism in our seemingly crime ridden world.

Where is the line that separates protection of the victim and protection of the individual's rights when accused of a crime?

The ensemble of characters we have grown to love is still present in this adventure, with Mary, the no-nonsense manager of Williams' Three Trails Hotel, becoming both a victim of a crime and a defendant in the same one.

There are the zany moments of the humor we have grown to expect from Thornhill, but there is also a more serious concern with society's moral issues that have become the focus of the story lines in his last few novels.

The added depth promotes these recent offerings from being just easy-read "cozy mysteries" to a more complex form of modern literature.

Can the Scales of Justice be balanced? Should they be?

Christina Fullerton Jones, Independence, Mo.

In *Lady Justice and the Vigilante*, Robert Thornhill has once again written another page turning installment in the Lady Justice series.

In *Lady Justice and the Vigilante*, the city of Kansas City is once again at the mercy of some unsavory characters that cause one man to take matters into his own hands as the criminals keep getting away with their crimes.

He becomes known as the vigilante and helps dispose of these criminals in his own manner.

While the reader comes to understand what has driven this man to this point, we are also faced with the dilemma of while he is ridding the town of criminals who have caused pain to many people, is he doing the right thing?

According to the law he isn't, but in his heart, he believes that what he's doing is right.

Lady Justice and the Vigilante is another well-written novel by Mr. Thornhill.

If you have read any of the previous novels you will not be disappointed with this latest installment. Even if you haven't had the chance to read any of the other Lady Justice novels you will still find this novel hard to put down.

I recommend this novel to any reader who enjoys crime stories and mysteries.

Michelle Castillo, Article Write Up

Walt Williams and his gang are back.

It seems a citizen is taking the law into his own hands and criminals are suddenly found murdered.

The public seems to be split on cheering on this vigilante or wanting him brought to justice.

Adding to this, one of Walt's friends finds themselves in trouble trying to defend both home and self.

Soon Walt is on the search for the Vigilante, while trying to help his friend out of a legal bind.

Will Walt and the Gang get to solve this crime or will the vigilante prevail?

Robert Thornhill knows how to spin a suspenseful thought-provoking tale, with lovable characters, a bit of comedy and a lot of controversy and leaves you wondering what truly is right and what is wrong.

Everyone has an opinion and Mr. Thornhill really makes the reader think what would he do if he were in that situation.

Fantastic read.

Sheri Wilkinson, Princeton, IL.

LADY JUSTICE

AND

THE VIGILANTE

A WALT WILLIAMS
MYSTERY/COMEDY NOVEL

ROBERT THORNHILL

Lady Justice and the Vigilante
Copyright February, 2012 by Robert Thornhill
All rights reserved.

Published in the United States of America

Cover design by Peg Thornhill

1. Fiction, Humorous
2. Fiction, Mystery & Detective, General

PROLOGUE

"In all criminal prosecutions, the accused shall enjoy the right to a speedy and public trial, by an impartial jury of the State and district wherein the crime shall have been committed, which district shall have been previously ascertained by law, and to be informed of the nature and cause of the accusation; to be confronted with the witnesses against him; to have compulsory process for obtaining witnesses in his favor, and to have the Assistance of Counsel for his defense." - U.S. Constitution 6th Amendment

In the Declaration of Independence Thomas Jefferson had written that *"all men...are endowed by their Creator with certain unalienable rights...[and] to secure these rights, governments are instituted.*

"When a government protects the rights of its people and provides an adequate remedy for those whose rights have been violated, then that government is providing equal justice for all.

"Justice requires an opportunity and a place to complain of an injury as well as the machinery to provide a remedy. For the accused, justice requires the opportunity to hear and understand the charge, cross-examine those who are making the charge, have a fair and speedy trial, and have an opportunity to repair the wrong if found guilty."

The notion of equal justice under the law was one of the fundamental principles of our founding fathers.

Our entire legal system is based on finding a balance between two, often opposing ideologies.

On the one hand, our system provides for the prosecution and punishment of those who break the law.

On the other hand, the same system provides those accused, a means to prove their innocence and equally as important, it provides protection for those who have been falsely accused.

Lady Justice, the symbol of our judicial system is depicted wearing a blindfold and holding a balance scale.

In a perfect world, the scales stay balanced. The guilty are prosecuted, found guilty and punished and the innocent are set free.

But it is not a perfect world.

English jurist, William Blackstone wrote, *"Better that ten guilty persons escape than one innocent suffer."*

Most of us would agree with that philosophy if we put ourselves in the shoes of the innocent who had been falsely accused.

But what about the victims of the ten guilty who see their rapist or mugger walk away scott free?

Where is the justice for them?

The organization, Victims And Citizens Against Crime, point out that six million Americans will become victims of violent crime this year.

Jonathan Swift wrote, *"Laws are like cobwebs, which may catch small flies, but let wasps and hornets break through."*

It is inevitable that when some criminal upsets the delicate balance of the scales of justice, slips through the loopholes of the legal system and walks away from his crimes with impunity, there will be one who takes to heart the admonition of Edmund Burke. *"All that is necessary for the triumph of evil is for good men to do nothing."*

CHAPTER 1

Ed Jacobs sat in the back of the courtroom quietly awaiting the return of the twelve men and women who would decide the fate of twenty-seven year old LeShawn Grimes.

He had been charged with breaking and entering, armed criminal action, grand theft and rape.

On the night of June 25th, 2011, a masked gunman had gained entry into the home of Ronald and Beth Martin by breaking the glass adjacent to the back door of the home and reaching in to unlock the door.

The intruder had surprised the Martins who were watching TV in the basement family room.

He immediately immobilized Ronald Martin by striking him in the head with his gun.

He bound the Martins' hands with plastic ties and proceeded to rummage through the house looking for valuables.

The Martins' seven-year-old daughter, Amanda, who was awakened by her mother's screams, hid under a pile of clothing in the laundry room.

Ronald Martin regained consciousness in time to see the intruder assault his wife before he fled the home.

Upon hearing the intruder leave the house, Amanda ran to the window and watched as the masked gunman drove away in a blue sedan.

Amanda freed her parents who immediately called 911.

Officers were on the scene within minutes and immediately radioed all police cruisers in the area to be on the lookout for a blue sedan.

A dozen blocks away, rookie officer Dwayne Bellows spotted a blue sedan that he pursued with lights and siren blazing.

The sedan pulled to the side of the road and Officer Bellows approached and asked the driver to produce his license and registration and he promptly complied.

Officer Bellows called in the license and was informed that LeShawn Grimes had an arrest record for several misdemeanors, but there were no outstanding warrants.

Officer Bellows asked Grimes where he had been and where he was going. Grimes replied that he had been with friends and was on his way home.

At that point, Grimes demanded to know why he had been stopped and detained and if he had broken any laws.

When the officer responded that he had not observed him breaking any laws, Grimes demanded the return of his license.

At that point, Officer Bellows examined the interior of the car and seeing nothing suspicious, ordered Grimes to open the trunk.

Grimes refused and Officer Bellows pulled the keys from the ignition and opened the trunk where he found a ski mask, plastic ties, assorted valuables that were later identified by the Martins and a snub-nosed revolver.

Officer Bellows drew his weapon, cuffed Grimes and radioed for assistance.

The case should have been a slam-dunk.

Quite the contrary.

Defense attorney Suzanne Romero represented LeShawn Grimes.

Romero had been a thorn in the side of the police department for years. Many a defendant had walked away free as she doggedly rooted out procedural errors in the police department's investigation.

Everyone from street cop to the chief himself knew that they had better have their ducks in a row if Suzanne Romero was at the defense table.

This case was no exception.

Officer Dwayne Bellows had taken the stand and the prosecutor was about to present all of the incriminating evidence that was found in the trunk of the sedan, when Romero objected.

The basis of the objection was that the search of the trunk was an unlawful search and violated Grimes' Fourth Amendment rights against unlawful search and seizure.

A pitched battle raged between Romero and the prosecuting attorney, each citing court cases to support their position.

In the end, the winning argument came from Romero citing Justices Brennan, Marshall and Stevens, *"In sum then, individuals accosted by police on the basis merely of reasonable suspicion have a right not to be searched, a right to remain silent, and, as a corollary, a right not to be searched if they choose to remain silent."*

The final nail in the prosecutor's coffin was when she cited Boyd v. United States. *"Where property or evidence has been obtained through unconstitutional search and seizure, failure to return the same and to suppress the evidence learned thereby constitutes a reversible error."*

The judge ruled Bellows' search to be unlawful and suppressed the incriminating evidence found in the trunk --- the fruit of the poisoned tree.

The intruder had worn a ski mask and gloves and left no trace evidence in the house.

Without the contents of the trunk, the prosecution was left with nothing to tie Grimes to the crime but a seven-year-old girl's testimony that she had seen a blue car drive away.

The jury had been out only a half hour when the bailiff notified the judge that they had reached a verdict.

Ed Jacobs watched Ronald and Beth Martin as the jury filed in.

He lived on the same street as the Martins, about ten houses to the south.

While not close friends, they had lived in the same neighborhood for a dozen years and were more than just casual acquaintances.

He had seen little Amanda grow up and his pantry was loaded with cookies from her various fund raising projects.

Ronald had his arm around his wife holding her close, hoping for the best but expecting the worst.

The courtroom was deathly silent as the judge took the slip of paper with the jury's verdict from the bailiff.

He turned to the defense table. "Will the defendant please rise."

Then to the jury, "Mr. Foreman, have you reached a verdict?"

"Yes, Your Honor. We have.

"What say you?"

"In the matter of the State of Missouri vs. LeShawn Grimes, we find the defendant not guilty on all charges."

The judge turned to Grimes, "Mr. Grimes, you are free to go."

Grimes let out a whoop and pumped his fists into the air.

As he was leaving, he stopped in front of the Martins.

A malicious grin spread across his face as he blew a kiss and winked at Beth Martin.

Beth buried her face in her husband's chest and burst into uncontrollable sobbing.

Ronald Martin watched in disbelief as the man who had broken into his home, struck him in the head and violated his wife walked cockily out of the courtroom.

Suzanne Romero gathered her papers and tucked them in her briefcase.

As she passed by the Martins, Ronald lashed out, "How can you defend garbage like that?"

Romero didn't respond or acknowledge the outburst. Whatever she was feeling was well hidden as she exited the courtroom followed by the disgusted stares of the onlookers.

Ed Jacobs sat in stunned silence as he watched the drama play out before him.

He had expected the not guilty verdict but as he watched the mocking smile and knowing wink of the rapist, he felt something grow inside of him that he had never felt before.

The feeling increased in intensity as he watched his neighbor and friend weeping in the arms of her husband.

He had the urge to scream at the top of his lungs --- a primal scream that would vent his pent-up feelings of frustration and helplessness.

He could feel the blood rushing to his head and he grabbed the seat of the wooden bench to keep from leaping to his feet.

Suddenly it dawned on him that the emotion he was feeling was RAGE --- pure unadulterated RAGE.

He wanted more than anything to grab Grimes around the throat and choke him until he was dead.

He wanted justice --- or was it revenge --- for the pain this animal had inflicted on his friends.

The courtroom began to empty and as he watched the people file out, he saw the pain and frustration in their faces as well, and knowing he was not alone helped him control the fire in his gut.

He composed himself as best he could and made his way to the Martins.

Beth's sobs had subsided and they simply sat there holding onto each other.

Ed put his hand on Ronald's shoulder and simply said, "I'm so sorry."

As Ed Jacobs drove home, he couldn't shake the vision of LeShawn Grimes pumping his fists in victory.

During the course of the trial, Grimes had shown no remorse and Ed had seen the vacant stare of a man without a soul.

Grimes was a sociopath pure and simple and now he was free to inflict more misery on innocent victims.

The rage he had initially felt had morphed into something more manageable, more controllable.

His rage had become resolve.

Ed Jacobs had always been a man of action.

As a youth fresh out of high school he had signed on as a carpenter's apprentice and over the course of ten years had learned the construction business from the ground up.

At the relatively young age of twenty-eight, he invested everything he owned into his own construction company.

Through hard work and determination his business prospered.

In 1995, he took another leap of faith and bought a parcel of farmland on the outskirts of Independence, Mo. about ten miles east of Kansas City.

He was counting on the development of the Little Blue Parkway to fuel interest in his new subdivision.

His gamble paid off better than he could ever have suspected.

He rode the wave of the housing boom from 2000 through 2005.

Unlike many of his competitors, he could see the writing on the wall and knew the bubble was about to burst.

In 2007, he cut the price to the bone on his last two speck homes and retired.

For two years, Ed and Martha, his wife of thirty-five years, traveled and enjoyed the fruits of his many years of hard work.

Then suddenly, Martha was taken from him by an unexpected illness and he found himself alone.

Ed and Martha had one son, Ed, Jr.

He was a bright kid and Ed gave him all of the advantages that a successful businessman could provide --- everything that is, but his time.

Ed spent long hours at his construction sites and his weekends were spent meeting deadlines instead of at little league games.

Ed, Jr. went off to college where he met the girl who was to become his wife.

He graduated with a degree in computer science and moved to the Silicon Valley in California.

The strong emotional ties that bind many fathers and sons just weren't there and when Martha died so did the bonds that held the family together.

Ed and his son stayed in touch at first, but as time passed the contacts grew farther apart.

After one brief conversation, Ed recalled the words to the old Harry Chapin song, *The Cats In The Cradle.*

And as I hung up the phone it occurred to me
He'd grown up just like me. My boy was just
like me

Ed Jacobs was alone.

His career was over.

At the age of sixty-five he had no goals or dreams, nothing to make him jump out of bed in the morning and greet the new day with enthusiasm and purpose.

Nothing --- until now.

On that long drive from the courthouse to his home, the rage that had become resolve, suddenly took on form and substance.

As he drove, he felt an excitement growing inside him that he hadn't felt in years.

By the time he pulled into his garage, all of the qualities that had driven Ed Jacobs over the years, all of the drive that had made him successful were awakened and focused on one goal.

Ed Jacobs knew what he had to do.

Ed was meticulous and thorough.

As a young finish carpenter, he had learned the virtues of patience and careful planning.

The miters in his crown molding were so precise it looked like one continuous piece of wood.

He knew if he was going to embark on this new journey, he must prepare or he would fail.

What he was contemplating was so far removed from his past life he hardly knew where to begin.

Then one day as he was researching related topics on the Internet, there was a reference to a movie he remembered seeing years ago, *Death Wish*.

The 1974 movie starred Charles Bronson as Paul Kersey, an architect whose wife had been brutally murdered and whose daughter had been raped.

When police efforts to apprehend the attackers produced no results, Kersey took matters into his own hands and began a vendetta against the criminal element of New York.

Ed rented the movie at Blockbuster and was spellbound as he watched Paul Kersey wage his personal war against crime.

After watching it once, he rewound it and watched it a second time taking detailed notes.

The rage and resolve that Kersey felt after the brutal assault of his family, mirrored his own feelings as he watched LeShawn Grimes make a mockery of the justice system.

He was surprised at the satisfaction and sense of fulfillment he experienced as he watched Kersey blow away the scum of New York.

But the thing that he noticed most was that Kersey made mistakes --- at lot of them that resulted in him being injured and becoming the focus of a police investigation into the random killings.

While Ed wanted justice and maybe even revenge, he certainly didn't want to wind up in jail or even worse, stabbed or shot.

He vowed not to make the same mistakes that Paul Kersey had made.

He believed with all his heart that what drove Grimes to commit the atrocities could not be fixed.

He had come to terms with the fact that LeShawn Grimes must die.

He just had to do it smarter.

He made a list of the mistakes that Kersey had made.

When the killings started, police looked for family members of victims of recent crimes.

That certainly made sense, but he was not a part of the Martin's family and really, not even a close friend. He should be all right there.

The cops knew that the vigilante was a good shot and immediately looked for family members with military backgrounds.

Ed's age made him one of the 'in-between-ers'. He was too young for the Korean War and too old for Vietnam. He had never served in the military.

So far, so good.

Next, the police narrowed the search to men living in the geographical area where the victims were shot.

Fortunately, Grimes had come across town to do his dirty work and when he would die, it would be on his own turf, not the Martin's neighborhood.

Kersey roamed the city streets in his fancy clothes, using himself as bait.

Ed had no intention of being close to any of these scumbags.

At the age of sixty-five, he was a fit one hundred and eighty pounds, but he didn't kid himself into believing he was a match for a twenty year old dope head high on PCP.

Kersey's killings were random, but he used the same .32 revolver each time, tipping the police that they were dealing with a single shooter.

Ed had some weapons, but he knew he must get more.

Kersey didn't bother to hide his identity and it was inevitable that there would be a witness to identify him.

Ed knew that he must become a master of disguise.

Ed's first stop was his basement storeroom.

He knew that somewhere amid the boxes of old books, Christmas decorations and photo albums there was a gun case containing his old deer rifle.

He had been an avid hunter in his youth, but once he started his own construction company there had been no time for such frivolity.

On the shelf that held the gun case, he also found his old metal cartridge box filled with cartridges and his Hoppes gun cleaning kit.

As he unzipped the case and felt the cold steel of the barrel, memories of the hunts on his grandfather's farm flashed in his mind.

He remembered the pride he had felt when he bagged his first deer and his grandpa's look of approval when he had nailed the coyote that had been eating his chickens.

This time, he would be hunting game of a more deadly nature.

The years in the basement had taken their toll and the blue-steel barrel was covered with a fine coat of rust.

He found rags and steel wool and with the solvent and oil in his kit, went to work.

The old gun was a Japanese 6.5 mm bolt action that he had bought at a used gun store fifty years ago.

He had looked at the more expensive Winchesters and Remington's, but the old World War II relic was all he could afford.

Now he was glad.

The old gun would be untraceable.

Next, he thought about how to hide his identity.

He shopped several thrift stores and picked out clothing that was totally foreign to his usual wardrobe, including several hats of different styles.

His last stop was the Kansas City Costume Company at 20th and Grand.

He left with a bag containing mustaches, beards eyebrows and wigs of various colors.

As he was driving home, he thought of the bags of old clothing and disguises and especially the rifle.

In the unlikely event that something unknown and unforeseen should lead the police to his door, these things should not be on the premises.

He headed to a public storage facility that he knew on Holmes Road and rented a 5 x 10 unit at the back of the lot.

Over the next few days, he equipped the unit with an old second hand dresser and mirror that he had picked up at a garage sale, a battery powered lantern and a small kerosene heater.

This would be his base of operations.

When he was certain that he had everything he needed to complete the task at hand, he was ready for the next phase --- find LeShawn Grimes.

It wasn't as if he was starting the search completely cold.

The trial had garnered a great deal of publicity and newspaper articles written by investigative reporters told of Grimes usual haunts.

Grimes stomping grounds was reported to be the Paseo corridor between Independence Avenue and Truman Road.

His mother lived in the Charlie Parker Square apartments at 12th and Paseo, and Grimes was known to frequent the bars and dives along Independence Ave.

Ed's first trip to the area was an eye opener.

Small groups of young thugs lounged in doorways and alleys and hookers paraded their wares under the dim streetlights.

He soon discovered that his shiny 2010 Lexus drew way too much attention and he beat a hasty retreat.

The next day he found a turd-brown 1994 Toyota Corolla on Craig's list for $1,400.00.

After a bit of haggling, he drove it away for $1,000.00 cash.

The next night, he dressed in clothing appropriate for the owner of such a vehicle and with a ball cap pulled low on his head cruised Independence Avenue looking for his prey.

On the third night, he spotted him leaving A J's Bar.

Grimes climbed into the car of a friend and Ed followed them to the Charlie Parker Square apartments.

Grimes entered the building and by two A.M. it was obvious that he was bunking, at least for now, with his mother.

Ed watched Grimes for a week and the same pattern was repeated night after night with Grimes arriving at the apartment at varying times.

Ed had driven every block around the apartment numerous times and as he surveyed the lay of the land, a plan began to take form.

The Paseo was a divided roadway with a twenty foot wide green strip separating the north and southbound lanes.

Concrete pillars joined by a three-foot concrete fence had been constructed in the green strip to form a grotto of sorts.

Undoubtedly, the original intention of this structure was for artistic purposes, but the floor of the grotto was littered with cigarette butts and beer cans and the columns were covered with graffiti.

Traffic was sparse along Paseo at the hours that Grimes returned to the apartment and Ed figured he could lie on the floor of the grotto in the shadows.

He could park the old Toyota a half a block away on a side street and be out of the neighborhood before anyone could call the cops.

He had made the preparations.

He had done his homework.

He had formulated a plan.

Now all that was left was the execution.

In the days after the trial, after his initial passion had cooled, Ed thought long and hard about what he was about to do.

He wasn't a violent man. He had never even struck another human being in anger.

Although he had been a hunter and killed rabbits, squirrels and deer, his desire to hunt had waned over the years and as he grew older, the taking of life had lost its appeal.

Now, he was contemplating taking the life of another human being.

Though not a religious man by nature, Ed had a strong sense of right and wrong and his moral compass had always been pointed in the right direction.

More than once he was ready to chuck the whole idea, but then the image of Grimes mocking poor Beth Martin would fill his head and his resolve would become even stronger.

In lighter moments, he compared what he was about to do to skydiving.

You could take classes. You could learn to pack a parachute. You could even go up in the plane, but at anytime up until that moment when you step out into the void, you could call the whole thing off.

Once you leap, there is no turning back.

Ed thought of this as he made his final preparations.

It was not too late.

He could sell the old Toyota. He could give the clothing back to the thrift store and put the rifle back on the basement shelf.

Once he pulled the trigger, there would be no turning back.

The next day Ed spent the morning pouring over family photo albums.

Pictures of himself and Martha enjoying the last years of their life together brought tears to his eyes.

He missed her so much.

He knew that he would do anything to bring her back. He knew that he would gladly give his life for her.

As he looked into her happy eyes in the photos, he wondered how he would feel if it had been Martha and not Beth Martin who had been ravaged at the hands of LeShawn Grimes.

He wondered how many more women would be scarred for the rest of their lives because this sociopath had slipped through the cracks of the legal system.

With a calm assurance he had not felt before, he placed the albums back in their boxes and climbed into the old brown Toyota.

By eleven o'clock, Ed was lying on his stomach peering through the uprights in the concrete fence.

The 6.5 mm was lying by his side.

He calculated that the shot would be about fifty yards. He had certainly made longer ones, but aiming through the shadows under the dim streetlights would be difficult.

He had no idea when or even if, Grimes would show up.

Patience was a virtue for a hunter.

He recalled his hunting days when he would get up hours before dawn and sit in his tree stand shivering in the bitter cold waiting for a buck to pass close enough for a shot.

This wait would be a piece of cake.

Once, he thought that the game was over when two young punks walked within twenty feet of where he was hiding, but they passed by, laughing and talking, totally unaware of his presence.

Finally, at one-thirty in the morning, a car pulled to the curb and LeShawn Grimes climbed out.

He shouted some parting words to the driver then leaned in and did one of those hand slapping, knuckle-knocking things that hoods do.

The car sped away and Grimes stood at the curb looking up and down the street.

Apparently he decided to have one last smoke before turning in and Ed saw him reach into his pocket and pull out a pack of cigarettes.

He saw the flare of the match and the glow of the ash as he inhaled deeply.

Then, in the glow of the streetlight Ed saw Grimes reach into his pocket again, only this time his hand held a small revolver.

He broke open the cylinder to check his load, and then snapped it shut and placed it back in his pocket.

As Ed Jacobs lined up his shot, he wondered how many people would be spared pain, degradation and humiliation at the hands of this animal because of what he was about to do next.

As he slowly squeezed the trigger he whispered, *"This is for you, Beth."*

LeShawn Grimes dropped to the ground and Ed Jacobs believed with all his heart that justice had been served.

CHAPTER 2

"Dirty Harry, of course! He was the best!"

That was the answer my partner, Ox, had given to the rhetorical question, 'who was the best cop ever'?

When the majority of your days are spent cruising the streets of Kansas City, rousting drunks and breathing exhaust fumes while directing traffic around an accident, you invent ways to pass the time and take your mind off the degenerate who had just puked in your back seat.

So, quite often, weighty subjects such as 'who was the sexiest woman' or 'where can you find the best pizza' filled the void in our humdrum day.

I realized that Ox had hit the nail on the head with the Clint Eastwood character and our conversation drifted to a rehash of Inspector Callahan's exploits.

"So what's your favorite Dirty Harry line?" I asked.

Ox thought for a minute, "It's gotta be the one where the bank robber is deciding whether Harry's gun is empty and Harry says, *'But being as this is a .44 Magnum, the most powerful handgun in the world, and would blow your head clean off, you've got to ask yourself one question: Do I feel lucky? Well, do ya, punk?'"*

"That was a good one all right," I replied, "but my favorite is when Harry's boss asked him how he knew the guy he took down was a perp and Harry answered, '*When a naked man is chasing a woman through an alley with a butcher's knife and a hard-on, I figure he isn't out collecting for the Red Cross!*'"

Ox roared, "A butcher knife and a hard-on! I'd forgotten about that one! Then there's always the classic, '*Go ahead, punk. Make my day!*'"

Hearing that line brought a smile to my face.

Mary Murphy, the seventy-three year old manager of my flophouse, the Three Trails Hotel, had used it more than once.

She had the sneer. She had the stare, and when she waved her thirty-six inch Hillrich & Bradsby baseball bat in the face of an obstinate tenant and spit out those words, he paid attention.

Ox's continued patter brought me out of my reverie. "Eastwood played some other cool characters. I loved him as Philo Beddoe in *Every Which Way But Loose*. That monkey he hung around with was a real hoot!"

"It wasn't a monkey. It was an orangutan."

"Picky, picky. And what about that goofy motorcycle gang? Do you remember what their name was?"

"Black Widows, I think. Yeah, I'm pretty sure it was the Black Widows."

Ox slowed the cruiser down to a crawl. "Speaking of motorcycle gangs, I wonder what's going down over there?"

We had been cruising Prospect Avenue and Ox was pointing to the Tool Shed Lounge, a known biker bar.

There were at least twenty Harleys lined up in the parking lot and one lone police cruiser.

"Do ya think we ought to check it out? Those odds don't look very good."

"Can't hurt," I replied. "It's not like we're on our way to something more important."

We parked the cruiser and entered the dim, smoky underbelly of the Tool Shed Lounge.

When our eyes had adjusted to the low light, we saw a lone officer weighing maybe a buck thirty, confronting a huge mountain of flesh twice the officer's size.

I whispered to Ox, "Isn't that Marvin Mercer?"

Ox squinted and then nodded, "Yep, that's Blackie!"

A year before, Ox and I had been assigned to serve a warrant on Marvin 'Blackie' Mercer.

The idiot had fled on his bike and we chased him for blocks before another cruiser blocked his path and he crashed into the bay of an Earl Shine paint shop.

Over the 'thump, thump' coming from the jukebox, we heard the officer bark. "Marvin Mercer, there's an outstanding warrant for your arrest. I'm taking you into custody. Turn around and place your hands behind your back."

Blackie stared incredulously at the figure before him, then suddenly burst into laughter.

"You seriously think you're gonna take me in? Look around, cop!"

The twenty or so bikers, resplendent in their leather, bandannas and chains had formed a big circle around the two.

A big fellow with a skullcap and greasy ponytail shouted, "Really, Marvin? You need our help to take down this scrawny cop?"

Blackie realized he was being baited and rose to the occasion. "Hell no! I'll pulverize the little punk!"

And without a moment's hesitation, he leaped forward and swung a fist as big as a ham directly at the head of the officer.

The officer ducked under Blackie's roundhouse and buried a fist into his flabby midsection.

The sound of the wind leaving the massive body echoed through the lounge quieting the laughter of the rowdy bikers.

Blackie grabbed his gut and staggered forward just as the officer planted a foot squarely into his crotch.

"Ohhhh, that's gotta hurt," Ox whispered.

The whimpering Blackie was obviously in a great deal of pain as he dropped to his knees.

The officer was on him in a flash and pushed him to the floor and was in the process of pulling his hands from his groin to apply the cuffs when the circle of bikers began to close in.

I saw that the situation had taken an ugly turn. "Oh no! This doesn't look good."

"Time to make our presence known," Ox replied.

In a booming voice that startled everyone in the room, including me, Ox bellowed, "Back off scumbags, unless you want to spend the afternoon downtown in lockup."

The bikers, seeing two more cops with their hands resting on their holstered weapons, began to back away.

Ox pulled his radio and held it high. "I'm calling for backup. In five minutes this place will be crawling with cops. I'm guessing Blackie wasn't the only guy in this room with an outstanding warrant. We'll have enough wagons to take you all in. My advice would be to clear out as fast as you can."

The bikers didn't need a second invitation. They bolted for the door and the rumble of the big Harleys coming to life and roaring down Prospect sounded like a summer thunderstorm.

When the room had cleared, the officer was pulling poor Blackie, who was still reeling from the nutcracker, to his feet.

"Nice work Officer --- uhhh," I said as we approached.

"DeMarco --- Judy DeMarco," she said turning in our direction.

We both stopped in our tracks and our mouths dropped open.

She removed her hat to wipe the beads of perspiration from her forehead and a mane of auburn hair cascaded over her shoulders.

Her high cheekbones, bright brown eyes and silky skin reminded me of a young Sophia Loren.

"Thanks for the backup. That might have gotten unpleasant if you guys hadn't shown up."

I was the first to find my tongue.

Ox just stood there staring like an idiot.

"What were you doing here by yourself? Where's your partner?"

"Frank got the squirts. I think maybe he got a hold of a bad tamale for lunch. I had to take him back to the station.

"The duty officer tried to find someone to ride with me, but no one was around. I just had a few more hours on my shift, so what the heck."

"So how did you end up in here?"

"I was cruising Linwood when I spotted this creep," she said, smacking Blackie in the back of the head.

"I thought there was a warrant out on him and dispatch confirmed, so I tailed him to the bar.

"Probably should have called for backup. I'll know better next time."

"You handle yourself pretty well."

"For a girl --- is that what you mean?"

"No, no. I meant no disrespect."

"I hear you. I get that all the time. I was the only girl with four older brothers. It was like the old Johnny Cash song, *A Boy Named Sue*. I had to either get tough or die."

She looked at Ox who was still just standing there staring with a silly grin on his face. "What's with your partner here? One minute he's scaring the shit out of a roomful of assholes and now all of a sudden he's deaf and dumb?"

"Ox!" I said, elbowing him in the ribs.

"Uhhh --- uhhh," was all he could manage.

"I have an idea," I said. "You've got to get Blackie back to the station and I don't think you should ride alone. How about Ox riding with you and I'll finish the shift by myself."

A look of abject terror spread across Ox's face and he started to shake his head.

Before he could respond, DeMarco winked at me and replied, "That would be great. This creep won't try anything with Mr. Tough Guy riding along."

I helped herd Blackie into the back of the cruiser and watched them drive away.

Ox still hadn't uttered a word.

I was hoping for a quiet evening at home but when I pulled up in front of my apartment building, I realized that just wasn't going to happen.

I live in a three story building on Armour Boulevard.

It originally was composed of two, two bedroom apartments on each floor.

This past year, I remodeled the whole top floor, making it one huge apartment for my new wife, Maggie, and me.

The other four apartments and a basement kitchenette are occupied by a strange assortment of individuals who I consider to be my closest friends and family.

All of them were huddled together on the front stoop.

My eighty-eight year old father was the first to speak as I trudged up the sidewalk.

"Sonny! Did you hear about the creep that was acquitted of the rape and break-in a few weeks ago?"

I'd heard about him, all right.

The guy had walked out of the courtroom a free man because a cop had screwed up.

It was a publicity nightmare. The press had been all over the case like a duck on a June bug and the department's reputation had taken a big hit.

Officer Dwayne Bellows was on administrative leave and word had come from the mayor's office that EVERYONE was to be reminded of proper investigative procedures.

Consequently, every officer had been required to spend remedial time at the academy.

"What about the guy?" I asked. "What has he done now?"

"He got himself shot, that's what." Dad replied.

Ox and I had been cruising all day and I didn't waste any time getting away from the station after completion of my shift, so this was certainly news to me.

"The bastard got what was coming to him. Anyone who rapes a woman in front of her husband deserves to die!"

That vindictive remark came from the lips of eighty-six year old Bernice Crenshaw, another long-time tenant and my dad's current love interest.

"Gosh, Bernice! Tell us how you really feel." As always, Jerry Singer, or 'Jerry The Joker' as we call our resident funny man, was ready with a quip or a zinger.

"Get over here and I'll do more than tell you how I feel," she shot back. "You just don't joke about rape!"

"Sorry," Jerry replied with genuine sincerity. "I wasn't thinking."

"So what happened?" I asked. "How about some details?"

My old friend and resident, Professor Leopold Skinner spoke up.

"LeShawn Grimes' body was found early this morning in front of his mother's apartment building at Twelfth and Paseo.

"He had one gunshot wound in his chest."

"Do they know who shot him? Are there any suspects?"

It was Willie's turn to contribute to the conversation.

"Dat's one rough neighborhood. Dey's drugs, prostitution, guns --- ever'ting over dere. Lots o' people been shot dere. It coudda been anybody."

Willie Duncan would know.

Before he became the maintenance man for my apartments, he had been a con man and roamed those very streets.

He had turned his life around and was now one of my closest friends.

"So what do you think?" Dad asked.

"What do I think about what?"

"The guy getting whacked. You're a cop. What do you think?"

"I think I've been working all day and I'm dog tired. I think I need to kiss my wife and sit down with a glass of Arbor Mist. As far as LeShawn Grimes is concerned, I don't think anything. It's not my case."

"Sheesh. I was just asking."

As I climbed the stairs to the third floor, I realized that what I had just said was not exactly true.

While I hated the fact that our city had suffered another homicide, way down deep inside I was glad that LeShawn Grimes was dead.

Maggie met me at the door.

After both of us living the single life for sixty-seven years, we tied the knot about six months ago.

We had been a 'couple' for many years and it finally dawned on us that there was so much more to gain by being married.

We had worked together at City Wide Realty until I hung up the old briefcase and got the wild hair to become a cop at the ripe old age of sixty-five.

Not many women could have or would have put up with such nonsense, but Maggie had supported me all the way.

"I see you passed though the gauntlet," she said, giving me a big hug and kiss.

"Yeah, everyone seems to be hyped up about this Grimes thing. I hadn't heard a word until I was surrounded by the Five Stooges down there."

"I'm surprised. It's all over the news."

"I'm sure I'll hear all about it at squad meeting tomorrow."

"So how was your day? Anything exciting?"

"Not really, other than Ox being smitten."

"Smitten! Is he okay?"

"No, no! Not like that. Smitten --- you know --- like in the romantic sense. I think Ox is in love."

Maggie broke into a big grin. "Tell me all about it."

After I shared the events at the Tool Shed Lounge, we compared notes on what we knew of Ox's love life.

Not much.

Ox was in his mid-forties; a twenty-four year veteran of the force and to my knowledge had never been within spitting distance of matrimony.

The big galoot was like a cuddly teddy bear until he got riled at which point he became a grizzly.

He was, by nature, a gentle, caring man and would have made some lucky girl a good husband.

Since I had known him, the closest Ox had come to a relationship was last summer.

I noted that we had been eating at Denny's more frequently than usual.

Then it dawned on me --- Ox was sweet on the waitress.

He finally worked up the nerve to ask her on a double date with Maggie and me. Unfortunately, it didn't turn out all that well.

We wound up being pursued by a religious nut in a humongous pick-up who tried to run us off the road.

After a high-speed chase over the Southwest Trafficway overpass, we managed to elude our pursuer, but Ox's poor date had been so frightened, she peed her pants.

On the way to her home, Ox asked if he could call her again, and to this day, I remember her words, "Ox, you're a great guy and I like you a lot, but your dates are just a little too intense for me. I think I'll pass."

I couldn't believe that any date would be too intense for Judy DeMarco.

"I hope this works out for Ox," I said. "I want him to know the same joy I feel every day with you."

I figured a few brownie points couldn't hurt.

"You're such a schmuck!"

41

CHAPTER 3

Ed Jacobs was glued to his TV set.

Every channel was carrying the story of the death of the villain who had escaped justice through a loophole in the law.

Eager reporters interviewed citizens on the street for their reaction and every one of them echoed the same sentiment. "He got what was coming to him."

The lone dissenter was LeShawn Grimes' mother.

Her hysterics filled the screen and she just kept screaming over and over, "My baby! My baby! Someone shot my baby!"

One reporter caught Grimes' defense attorney, Suzanne Romero, exiting the courthouse and shoved a camera in her face.

Her demeanor was the same as in the courtroom, stony and cold and she brushed by the reporter with a "No comment!"

The police department had held a press conference and in their usual fashion said a lot of words without really saying anything at all.

The official position was that they were treating this case no differently than any other homicide and that the department, as usual, was committed to solving all open cases.

At the moment there were no suspects or persons of interest and the motive for the slaying was unknown.

Ed had seen the news vans cluttering the streets in front of the Martin's home and was not surprised to see the faces of his friends on the tube.

Ron and Beth Martin were on the step in front of their home. Ron had his arm around his wife holding her close.

The reporters fired a barrage of questions their way and Ron simply raised his hand to silence them.

He had obviously been expecting this moment to come.

"We knew when we heard of the death of LeShawn Grimes that you people would be paying us a visit.

"We're not going to answer any questions, but we have prepared a statement for you."

He pulled a sheet of paper from his pocket and began to read.

"The events of the past few months have changed our family forever.

"No one --- my wife, my daughter, myself --- will ever fully recover from the horror we experienced on the night of June 25th.

"The tragedy was compounded further when the man who brought this misery to our door walked away a free man.

"I'm sure you want to know what we're feeling today. First, we're feeling regret that this incident ever happened and anger that the perpetrator escaped punishment for his crimes.

"I would be less than honest with you if I denied that today we also feel a great sense of relief

that this man will no longer be a threat to either my family or someone else's.

"We want to extend our sympathy to LeShawn Grimes' mother. We can certainly relate to the pain she is feeling today.

"With this turn of events, it is my hope that our family can now put this horrible chapter behind us and get on with our lives.

"Thank you."

Ed Jacobs turned off the TV and sat in silence, contemplating what he had just seen.

During the planning phase of Grimes' death, he was so filled, first with rage and then resolve, he was convinced that what he was doing was right.

On the day of the actual event, he was riding the high that was induced by excitement, fear and adrenalin.

Secretly, he wondered if after the deed was done and the adrenalin had dissipated, when he faced the cold reality that he had taken the life of another human being, he would be wracked with regret and remorse.

The time had come to face that reality.

After seeing the relief of Ron and Beth Martin and hearing the remarks from the citizens on the street, he realized that what he was feeling was not unlike the time he and Martha had purchased food and clothing for a needy family and donated them anonymously.

It was a feeling of accomplishment; a feeling of giving and expecting nothing in return; it was a feeling of making someone's life better as a result of your actions.

He liked the feeling.

Now it was decision time.

Was this to be an isolated event that had served its purpose or maybe something more --- maybe the beginning of a new phase in the life of Ed Jacobs?

He thought about his existence before 'the event'.

He was retired, he was alone and his life had no purpose or meaning.

He just existed --- was just treading water.

Since the first day 'the event' began to take shape in his mind, he had greeted each new day with enthusiasm and felt a sense of urgency and fulfillment that he hadn't felt for years.

He recalled a comic strip from the morning's *Kansas City Star*.

A grandmotherly woman was speaking to her granddaughter and said, "People all over the world are in need and I'm at an age where I can help out a little."

The youngster responded with, "Yeah, old age!"

The senior's reply was, "Yup! Lots to give, not much to lose!"

That was what Ed Jacobs was feeling.

Lots to give, not much to lose.

Reading the *Star* every morning also gave Ed the realization that he would never have to look very far to find the next piece of human garbage that needed to be dumped.

Every day there was page after page reporting murders, rapes and carjacking.

The perps were like cockroaches that roam the streets at night defiling the lives of the innocent people they touch, and like the cockroaches, they needed to be exterminated.

Lots to do, not much to lose.

Ed Jacobs was ready to get to work.

CHAPTER 4

As I had suspected, the main topic of discussion at squad meeting the next morning was the shooting of LeShawn Grimes.

Captain Short brought us up to date.

"This Grimes thing has turned into a media circus.

"The press hung us out to dry because we blew the investigation and let Grimes slip through the cracks.

"Now someone has offed the guy and everyone in town, except his mother, is saying 'good riddance'.

"It's still a homicide and we must still investigate. The best way to put this thing to bed is to find the shooter ASAP, and hope to God it was a drug deal gone bad or the work of a gang banger."

Officer Dooley raised his hand, "So are you ruling out the possibility that it's connected to someone associated with the trial?"

"We're not ruling out anything at this point.

"Our first suspect was, of course, Ronald Martin, the victim. The Medical Examiner puts the time of death between midnight and three a.m. According to Beth Martin's mother who had been staying with them during the ordeal, all the family were at home all night."

Another officer raised his hand, "Anything from ballistics?"

"Yes, and it certainly muddies the waters."

"The slug that killed Grimes was from a 6.5 mm rifle, probably Italian or Japanese, dating back to World War Two."

"Geesh, who uses a gun like that and where would somebody get one?"

"Deer hunters mostly. They can be picked up at used gun stores or somebody could have brought one home from the war as a souvenir.

"Today, we hit the streets. We know that Grimes hung out on Independence Avenue. We're going to canvass the Avenue from downtown to Prospect and for three blocks around the site of the shooting.

"Find out what Grimes was up to, who he talked to and where he went. Somebody had to see something.

"Your assignments are posted.

"Good luck!"

Ox and I picked up our assignments and on the way to the cruiser, I asked, "How'd it go with Blackie yesterday afternoon?"

"No problems. He was still in a world of hurt from DeMarco crushing his family jewels."

"Ah, yes, Miss DeMarco, or is it Mrs. DeMarco?"

"It's Miss."

"Really, and how do you know that?"

"I asked around."

"How come we've never run into her before?"

"She just transferred from the station north of the river. She's just been here a few days."

"What else did you learn about her on the drive back to the station?"

"I know she likes pizza."

"How did you discover that tidbit of information?"

"We were driving down Main and passed the Pizza Shack. She said she heard that was a really good place to get pizza."

"And?"

"And what?"

"Ox, you're a big doofus!"

I saw the perplexed look on the big guy's face.

"That was an engraved invitation for you to ask her out. So what did you say?

"I just said that I'd heard that too --- I messed it up, didn't I?"

"Let's just say that you're not off to a very good start."

That put Ox in a funk and he was quiet as we drove to our assignment.

Our job that day was to canvass Independence Avenue and try to find someone who had seen or had contact with Grimes on the night of his death.

We hit all the stores and watering holes along the Avenue, and as we expected, no one saw or heard a thing, or if they did, they weren't telling.

We were about to call it a day when we spotted three guys hanging in an alley by a liquor store.

They watched us warily as we approached.

"You guys know this fellow?" I asked holding up a picture of Grimes.

"Sho, we know 'em. Dat's one crazy messed up dude."

"What's your name?" Ox asked.

"Tyrone, what's yours?" he shot back as if he really cared.

"What exactly do you mean by 'messed up'?"

"De fool was always doing some kind of crazy shit; dumb stuff dat would'a got us in trouble fo' nuthin."

"Such as?"

"One night we was jus' cruising' and we went out to Independence. Dere on de square dey got a statue of Harry Ass Truman, you know, de ole president, and he's walkin' with a cane or something'.

"LeShawn jumps out o' de car and rips the cane right out of the guy's hand. Some ole lady saw him an' started screamin' bloody murder."

"Tell 'em about Jennifer Lopez," his friend said.

"Oh yeah, dat was really messed up.

"We was truckin' down I-70 and about Prospect, dere's a big billboard with Jennifer Lopez selling perfume or sum such shit.

"LeShawn parks de car right on the freeway an' gets a can o' spray paint from the trunk.

"Den he shinnys up de ladder and paints a big mustache right on Jennifer's face.

"JENNIFER LOPEZ, for chrissakes!"

It was obvious that Tyrone was more concerned with the welfare of Ms. Lopez than our esteemed president.

I tried to keep a straight face.

"So when was the last time you saw Grimes?"

"Saw 'em de night he got whacked. He had been hangin' at A J's an' I seen him leave and get in de car with Leon."

"Leon, who? What's his last name?"

"Hell, I don' know. Jus' Leon!"

"Do you know what time it was?"

"Bout one"

Except for Leon and, of course, the shooter, these were the last guys to see LeShawn Grimes alive.

We headed back to the station and filed our report.

We had clocked out and were heading to the parking lot when I saw Judy DeMarco unlocking her car.

I gigged Ox in the ribs and nodded my head in her direction.

In the two years that I had known Ox, he had been fearless in the face of danger, but I could see the terror in his eyes as he watched the lovely Ms. DeMarco across the parking lot.

"Well, what are you waiting for? Go on," I urged.

"But --- but!"

"But nothing!" I said, giving him a shove.

"Uhhhh --- Officer DeMarco. Do you have a minute?"

She looked up and gave him a smile. "Hi Ox. What's on your mind?"

"Well --- Uhhh ---- do you remember yesterday when you said you had heard the Pizza Shack was a pretty good place?"

"Ox, are you asking me for a date?"

I thought my old friend was going to drop a load.

"Well --- Uhhh --- yes! I guess I am."

"I wondered how long it would take you to grow a pair and ask me out."

She gave me a glance and a wink. "I suppose that grandpa here is coming along for moral support."

"Well, Walt and Maggie are my best friends. If you don't mind ---"

"Sure! The more the merrier."

"How about Saturday night? Pick me up at six. I live in one of those new loft apartments in the River Market District. Here's my address," she said, slipping him a piece of paper.

Ox just stood there with his mouth open.

"Oh, by the way, no more of this Officer DeMarco crap. My name is Judy."

Without another word, she climbed into her car and drove away.

I clapped my partner on the back.

"Nice work. I think you had her with 'Uhhhh'."

Ed Jacobs had found exactly what he was looking for.

He had searched the Internet and found an estate sale on a farm in a little town called Archie about an hour south of Kansas City.

Listed in the items to be auctioned were several guns.

Once Ed had decided to pursue his new venture, he was determined to take every precaution and not repeat the mistakes that Paul Kersey had made.

His first kill had been with the 6.5 mm and he needed a new weapon.

What he found was perfect, a Winchester 30.30 lever action with a scope.

This rifle, like his own, had probably been in the farmer's family for years and was untraceable.

He was able to get the rifle, a box of ammo and an old .22 caliber revolver that the owner had most likely used to plunk rabbits and squirrels.

He was ready to select his next target.

After watching the ten o'clock news, the choice was obvious.

A man armed with a knife had broken into the home of a seventy-one year old North Kansas City widow and raped her repeatedly over several hours.

A neighbor, hearing her screams, had called 911 and the man was apprehended fleeing the apartment.

Police reported that the suspect, Brian Larson, was also linked to the rape of a seventy-nine year old woman a week earlier.

The scene shifted from the news anchor to the North Kansas City police station where Larson was currently being held.

As the cuffed Larson was being ushered from the squad car to the jail, there was a moment when he looked directly into the camera.

Ed Jacobs saw that same vacant remorseless stare that he had seen in the eyes of LeShawn Grimes.

For Ed and probably anyone else, the very act of raping women of that age was utterly repulsive.

Most likely, Larson would be convicted and sentenced to five years, and with good behavior and given the crowded conditions in our prisons, be out on the streets in three.

Ed couldn't let that happen.

The news story ended by saying that on Saturday evening Larson would be transported downtown to be held in lock-up until his arraignment on Monday morning.

Ed pulled the old Toyota out of the garage and headed downtown.

He needed a plan.

Multi-storied buildings surrounded the downtown jail at 1300 Cherry; some were occupied, some not.

A half a block away, loud music blared from one of the old buildings and garish lights illuminated a queue of young people waiting their turn to enter.

Ed had forgotten that Halloween was just a few days away, and as was the custom for the past few years, many of the old vacant buildings had been rented and turned into spook houses.

Kids couldn't wait to pay ten bucks a pop to get the bejeezus scared out of them.

Ed watched the crowd and noted that about half of the revelers were in costume.

He also noted that from the roof of the old building, there was a clear view of the jail.

Ed found a parking spot a few blocks away and waited in line for his turn to enter.

He paid his fee and asked the guy at the door if there was a bathroom.

The guy said he thought there was one down the hall.

Instead, Ed found the stairway that led, floor by floor to the roof.

In the cool, crisp night air, Ed found the perfect spot for his ambush.

On the way home he stopped by one of the costume shops that pop up at Halloween each year and bought a set of army fatigues and a helmet.

On a night where hundreds of people would be in costume, he'd never be noticed.

When I told Maggie that we were double dating with Ox, she was thrilled.

Maggie is a romantic and the prospect of her giving cupid a helping hand set her all a twitter.

She concluded that to put Ox in the best light, he should drive, pick us up first and then get Judy.

We pulled up in front of her building and waited for Ox to make his move, but he just sat there frozen in time like the stone statues on Easter Island.

"Well, aren't you going to go get her?" Maggie asked.

Ox just gave her that 'deer in the headlights' stare.

"Oh for heaven's sake. She's not going to bite."

"I just don't want to mess up again. I really like her."

Maggie replied with a much softer tone, "Ox, you're a great guy. Just be yourself. Be the guy we know. That's all you have to do."

With that encouragement, Ox went forth with the same trepidation he must have felt on his first trip to the dentist.

Thank goodness Maggie and I were along.

Ox reminded me of an old fifties song, *I Got Tongue-Tied*, by the Rock-A-Billy Queen, Wanda Jackson.

When he walked up and said 'hi sweetie pie',
Well, all I could say was a neenie-neenie-ny
I got tongue-tied. Yeah, I got tongue-tied.

To her credit, Judy seemed to understand the situation and did her darndest to put Ox at ease and bring him into the conversation.

By the time the pizza hit the table, Ox seemed to have overcome his initial fear and was his usual lovable self.

Judy shared that she had been an army brat, constantly moving from one base to another and at the tender age of eighteen, had enlisted in the service.

After putting in her twenty as an MP, she came to Kansas City and joined the force.

Judy DeMarco was a complex woman.

She had the classic good looks of a Sophia Loren and a smile that would take your breath away, but underneath she was tough as nails.

She certainly wasn't someone I'd want to tangle with.

Just ask Blackie.

With her military training, she was quite knowledgeable about guns and that impressed the heck out of Ox.

They became engrossed in a conversation comparing the attributes of various weaponry, most of which I had never heard.

As we sat listening to this exchange, I detected a smile on Maggie's lips.

Apparently she and cupid were pleased with the way the evening was progressing.

After the last pizza crumbs had been consumed, Judy's eyes lit up.

"It's still early. You guys up for a little fun?"

"What did you have in mind?" I replied.

"Let's do a spook house!"

Maggie and I exchanged skeptical looks.

The last time we had been in one of those places, we had found a real dead body.

"Sounds like fun to me," Ox said. "There's one a half a block from the station. I'm in!"

Not wanting to be party poopers, we reluctantly agreed.

The line into the spook house stretched for a block down the street.

I hate waiting in lines --- always have.

I hate theme parks.

You stand in line for an hour to get a three-minute ride. It makes no sense.

No matter which line I pick at the grocery store, it's always the wrong one.

Every check out can have three people deep except the one I choose which has only one person ahead of me.

I unload my cart and inevitably I hear, 'price check on three' or 'I'm sorry ma'am, your credit card was denied'.

I'm the poster boy for Murphy's Law as it applies to waiting lines.

At least in this line, there was something to look at.

Maggie and I were probably forty years older than most of the other people in line.

About half were in costume and the other half might as well have been with all their piercing, studs and tattoos.

We saw likenesses of everyone from Lady Gaga to President Obama.

One young guy with glasses walked up to Judy and said "Good evening madam. My name is Potter, Harry Potter."

Judy's "Get lost, creep!" was enough to send the guy packing.

We were close to the ticket booth when I spotted a guy in army fatigues and helmet with a rifle slung over his shoulder.

I pointed him out to Ox and Judy.

"That looks like a real gun." I said.

Right behind him was a guy dressed as a buccaneer carrying a broadsword at his side. He was trying to mimic Johnny Depp playing Jack Sparrow in *Pirates Of The Caribbean.*

"So what are you?" Ox asked. "The costume police?"

At that moment a voice said, "You guys want a ticket, or not!"

I cringed as we shelled out forty bucks and headed to the inner sanctum.

There was the usual blood and gore and of course, all of the villains from zombies and vampires to Jason in his hockey mask.

Naturally, the air was filled with the screams of teenage girls clutching the arms of their boyfriends in mock terror.

Then, out of the blue, there was a sound that we hadn't heard before.

"CRAAAAACK!"

Judy stiffened.

"That was a rifle --- a real rifle."

She grabbed Ox's arm.

"Let's go!"

We fought the stream of revelers back to the entrance and peered down the hallway that led to the other parts of the big building.

At the far end of the hall, we saw a figure emerge from the stairwell.

"It's that army guy," I whispered. "The one with the rifle."

"Stop right there! "Ox bellowed. "Kansas City police!"

Naturally, the guy took off at a run. They always do.

As he turned the corner, we saw him pause and reach for the wall.

Instantly, a siren began to blast and overhead sprinklers came to life flooding everything.

I had seen newsreels of panicked partygoers fleeing burning nightclubs, but unless you've lived it, you couldn't understand the fear and chaos that ensued.

Mock screams of terror became real screams as everyone rushed for the door.

People fell, but no one stopped to help them up.

We were trapped in the human tide scrambling to escape, but knowing that there was no fire, we pushed through to the dark hallway.

We ran to the spot we had last seen the shooter, but around the corner an exit door stood open.

We looked in every direction, but he was long gone.

I looked at the four of us standing there panting and dripping wet.

It occurred to me at that moment that I was glad Ox's date was Judy DeMarco and not the gal from Denny's.

Ox's nights on the town are definitely intense.

CHAPTER 5

It was after midnight by the time order had been restored to the spook house and we had given our statements to the investigating officers.

We learned that the shot that we had heard had shattered the skull of Brian Larson, a perp that was being transported to lock-up for arraignment on Monday morning.

Larson had been accused of the rape of two elderly women.

It took every ounce of willpower to drag my butt out of bed the next morning.

Maggie and I usually hit the sack by ten o'clock and rarely make it to the sports report on TV before drifting off to sleep.

When I opened the *Kansas City Star*, I was shocked to read the headline, "POLICE BAFFLED BY VIGILANTE MURDERS!"

This was the first time I had seen the 'V' word mentioned.

The killing of LeShawn Grimes could have been viewed as an isolated incident, and given his shady background, any number of people could have been suspects.

But now, the extermination of two seemingly unrelated low-lifes in less than ten days, gave credence to the possibility that a vigilante was indeed roaming the streets of Kansas City.

I was dreading squad meeting.

Captain Short had already been under pressure from everyone up the chain of command, and as everyone knows, 'poop runs downhill'.

As I suspected, the Captain looked like 'he had been drug through a knothole backwards', as my grandma used to say.

I'm sure he had gotten a lot less sleep than I had.

When he addressed the squad, you could see that he was a man on the edge.

"Right in our own back yard! We lost a prisoner right in our own back yard! Blown away surrounded by cops! How does this happen?"

I wanted to tell him, and I'm sure others did too, that it wasn't anybody's fault and there was nothing anyone could have done to prevent the killing, but no one spoke.

He tried to compose himself.

"The papers are saying that this is the work of the same person that offed Grimes and that we are dealing with a vigilante.

"At this time, there is no evidence to support that theory.

"The slug that killed Larson was from a 30.30 and Grimes was killed with a 6.5 mm.

"If it is the same perp, he's being very careful to cover his tracks.

"All we have to go on at this point is the testimony of Officers Williams, Wilson and DeMarco who were at the scene and described the shooter as a male dressed in army fatigues."

He looked at the three of us.

"Anything else come to mind since you made your statements last night?"

We all shook our heads.

"We've got to put a lid on this thing. The last thing we need is some guy running loose in our town, making himself the judge, jury and executioner.

"Right now he's killing scumbags, but sooner or later, there's going to be an innocent victim.

"People just can't take the law into their own hands."

Ed Jacobs was also reading the headline in the *Star*.

He knew that it would come, but he was surprised that it had come so soon.

"Vigilante."

That was the word used in the papers, on TV and on the street.

As in the Grimes' shooting, the average man on the street had no sympathy for a criminal that had raped two women in their seventies. The world, it seemed to them, was a better place without him.

The American Civil Liberties Union weighed in with a different point of view.

"Law and order is the foundation of our society. Whether or not we are in agreement with every outcome, our civil liberties must be protected.

"LeShawn Grimes was found innocent by a jury of his peers and Brian Larson had not even been formally charged with a crime.

"Regardless of our personal feelings toward these men, the bigger issue is that they were deprived of their civil liberties.

"If we tolerate this miscarriage of justice, where do we draw the line?

"This murderer must be stopped. Vigilante justice must never be tolerated."

'Murderer', he hadn't really thought of himself in those terms.

He let it sink in for a moment.

Then he thought of the old proverb, *"You can please some of the people some of the time, but you can't please all of the people all of the time."*

Everyone was entitled to their opinions, but as Dirty Harry said, "Opinions are like assholes. Everybody's got one."

Then, his thoughts turned to something more urgent; he had almost been caught.

In spite of all his precautions, there was no way he could have known that off duty police would have been at the scene.

Thankfully, the sprinkler system had given him time to escape.

Without that diversion, he would never have outrun the cops.

He had arrived at his car totally winded and barely able to breathe. Maybe it was time to renew his membership at the YMCA.

Recent events had led him to believe that if he continued this course of action, it was inevitable that, sooner or later, he would be forced to defend himself.

He had seen a karate class advertised for older adults.

He had prepared himself mentally for the task ahead and now it was time to prepare physically, and even more important, he would have to be more careful next time.

The cops on the scene the night before had taken names, numbers and addresses on everyone that they could corral after the panic.

We were given a portion of the list and our day was spent following up with all those people, hoping someone knew something or had seen something, but we came up empty.

I was totally beat by the time the day was over. The lack of sleep and the day's fruitless search for clues had left me drained.

After supper, I was stretched out in front of the TV doing my darndest to keep my eyes open, when the phone rang.

Reluctantly, I picked up the receiver.

"Mr. Walt! This is Mary!"

"Hi Mary. What's up?"

"What's up is that we've been robbed!"

I put my pants back on, grabbed Willie from the basement apartment and we headed to the Three Trails Hotel.

This architectural monstrosity is the last remnant of my once large rental portfolio.

Finally growing weary of the hassles of being a landlord, I sold everything --- everything that is, except the Hotel. Nobody would touch it.

It's a flophouse, plain and simple.

There are twenty sleeping rooms containing a bed, dresser and chair and its occupants share four hall baths.

My tenants are a motley conglomeration of old guys on social security and younger guys working out of the labor pool.

The rent is forty dollars a week and most of the guys pay in cash.

Presiding over this rental anomaly is seventy-three year old Mary Murphy.

She lives in a one-bedroom apartment on the first floor.

There is a mail slot in her door where the tenants deposit their weekly rent.

Due to their irregular working schedules, rent could be deposited at any hour of the day or night.

When we walked on to the porch, we could see that Mary was in a dither.

"Oh, Mr. Walt. We've been burgled."

Willie leaned over and whispered, "Where'd she get dat word?"

I just shook my shoulders.

"What happened, Mary?"

"I decided to go out for the evening. I had me a burger at the Dairy Bar and took in the early movie. When I got home, the door was busted in."

Sure enough, the doorframe had been splintered.

"Can you tell if anything was taken?"

"Nothing except some of the rent money. I noticed that there were a couple of envelopes in the box under the slot when I left. I figured I would take care of them when I got home. Guess I shoulda done it before I left. I'm sorry, Walt."

"Any idea how much there might have been or who had put it through the slot?"

At that moment, I noted that the porch had filled with most every tenant in the building.

One old guy raised his hand. "Mine was in there."

As soon as the words were out of his mouth, there arose a chorus.

"Me too!" "Me too!" "Me too!"

It seemed that mysteriously, everyone had paid their rent this week during the three hours that Mary was at the movies.

Since there was no way I could prove otherwise, I had no choice but to write off the whole week as a loss.

"Willie can you secure this for the night?"

"Sho 'nuff. Den I'll come back tomorrow an' fix it proper."

I assured Mary that everything would be OK and ushered her into her apartment.

I was bone tired and I was pissed that I had lost a week's rent, but more than anything, I was angry that some creep had violated my building and Mary's home.

I didn't mean for it to happen, but suddenly the thought popped into my head.

"Maybe the vigilante will bust a cap in his ass!"

CHAPTER 6

Although the media was wringing as many headlines and sound bites from the vigilante case as possible, and the department had made the apprehension of the shooter a top priority, other cases and other criminals could not be ignored.

At squad meeting, the Captain introduced Sergeant Winkler from the drug task force.

"As you all know, the production and sale of illegal drugs in our city is an ongoing battle.

"One of our most effective deterrents is the honest citizens of the community who suspect suspicious activity in their neighborhoods and report it to the task force.

"We are working on one such case now.

"There have been numerous reports of suspicious activity in an eastside neighborhood, an increase of traffic on the residential streets late at night, strangers walking the streets and veiled threats to homeowners to 'mind their own business'.

"We have narrowed the activity to a home in the twenty-seven hundred block of Myrtle.

"Our plan is to sweep the block, house by house, with the aid of an old friend of mine."

Winkler gave a whistle and a beautiful chocolate Labrador retriever trotted into the room.

"This is Buster and he's got a nose you wouldn't believe. Let me show you.

"Before the meeting, I taped a joint to the bottom of one of your chairs. Let's see if Buster can find it."

Winkler made a hand signal and nodded his head and Buster made the rounds of the room huffing and puffing like a freight train.

When he reached my chair, he sat on his haunches, looked me in the eye and snorted, "Rufffff!"

"Officer," Winkler said, "you're under arrest for possession of a controlled substance."

Then he barked an order. "Buster! Hold!"

The lab rose to his feet and his big head went straight for my crotch. Before I knew it, my privates were being held firmly in his jaws.

My fellow officers, seeing the horror written across my face, laughed uncontrollably.

"Officer, I wouldn't make any sudden movements," Winkler admonished.

This was my second encounter with a police dog.

The first was a German Shepherd who had obviously had the same training as Buster, since he too had become intimate with Mr. Winkie and the boys.

Finally, after what seemed an eternity, Winkler barked, "Release! Come!"

Buster and I parted company and he trotted to his master's side.

Dooley couldn't pass up the opportunity to deliver a zinger.

"Hey, Walt! Does Maggie know you're into this animal thing? If she doesn't she soon will!"

"*Lucky me!*" I thought.

When order was restored, Winkler continued.

"We don't want to give Buster any preconceived notions by leading him directly to the suspect house, so we're going to let him sniff every home on the block and draw his own conclusions.

"The reason I'm here is that we need some extra manpower to cover the neighborhood.

"While Buster and my officers are sniffing around, we need some of you to cover the rear of the houses in case someone tries to rabbit on us.

"I could use four guys."

Then he looked at me.

"How about you and your partner, seeing as how you and Buster are already acquainted?"

I looked at the Captain and he nodded his head while trying to stifle a smile.

I turned to Ox. "Well partner, I guess we're on dog duty."

We parked the four cruisers a block away from the target street and set out on foot.

Winkler freed Buster from his leash and the big dog trotted off with his nose in the air.

The task force guys stayed close to Buster as he went house to house and Ox and I and two other officers headed for the back yards.

There was an old alley that ran between the back of the houses being searched and the rear of the houses on the next block.

Ox and I stayed close to the houses and the other two guys covered the alley.

It was slow going.

Buster was thorough and sniffed the perimeter of each house before moving on.

We all knew which house was the target house and when Buster started sniffing, we were all ready for anything.

Sure enough, Buster lit up like a Geiger counter and Winkler gave the signal that we had pinpointed the drug house.

The plan was that once Buster had detected drugs, Winkler would radio back to the station where an officer was waiting to get a judge's signature on a search warrant.

An assault team would deliver the warrant and storm the house.

It took the better part of a half hour before the assault team showed up with the warrant.

The back of the house had a basement garage and a gravel driveway that led to the alley.

I was between the back door and the garage and Ox was on the other side of the garage door by the corner of the house.

We heard Winkler pound on the front door and bellow, "Police! Open up! We have a warrant to search the premises!"

We heard no response from the front of the house, but from behind the basement door we heard the distinct rumble of a Harley coming to life.

The guy was going to roar out of that basement on his bike and it looked like our only choices were to either shoot him or let him get away.

I knew I certainly wasn't going to stand in front of the big machine and I hoped Ox wouldn't.

Then I saw it.

A fifty-foot garden hose was coiled under an outside water faucet.

I grabbed the hose and uncoiled enough of it to reach across the driveway.

I figured I had time for one throw before the guy came roaring out.

I pitched the hose like a lifeguard throwing a ring and Ox grabbed the end as the garage door swung open.

We heard the engine rev up and the guy came flying out the door.

I braced my hundred and forty-five pounds against the back of the house, but when the perp hit the hose it nearly jerked my arms out of their sockets.

The perp flipped into the air and landed flat on his back and the Harley crashed into the fence on the far side of the alley.

Winkler and the rest of the crash team came rushing around the house.

When they saw the perp lying unconscious under a green garden hose, they all applauded.

Buster came trotting up to me and licked my hand.

What more could a guy ask for?

The drug dealer was Damien Price.

A search of the home found a working meth lab in the kitchen and a hundred and twenty live marijuana plants being cultivated under grow lights in the basement.

We had taken down one of the biggest drug dealers in Kansas City.

The department had been crucified in the press for the Grimes screw-up and its' inability to catch the vigilante, so they wasted no time in making the bust front-page news.

A picture of Winkler and Buster accompanied a heartwarming article about man's best friend aiding in the war against crime.

The department needed a slam-dunk.

They couldn't have scripted a better one.

Price was being held in County lock-up until his arraignment.

Because, technically, Ox and I had collared the perp, we had been subpoenaed to appear in court.

Lights, cameras and on-the-spot reporters lined the stairway leading into the courthouse and clogged the hallways.

It was standing room only inside the courtroom.

Even though the case had generated a lot of interest and Buster had won the hearts of the community, it seemed that all this attention was a bit overboard.

A bailiff led us to our seats and when I looked at the defense table, I realized why this case was the center of attention.

The defense attorney was none other than Suzanne Romero.

Romero rarely lost a case and why she would represent a douche bag like Price, especially in a trial where the outcome was a foregone conclusion, was a mystery.

The chatter in the courtroom ceased when the bailiff announced in his big boy voice, "Hear ye! Hear ye! This court is now in session, the Honorable Franklin Bush presiding. All rise!"

Suddenly I had a hollow feeling in the pit of my stomach.

Judge Bush, while fair, was known as a liberal and quite the antithesis of a hanging judge.

Now, with Suzanne Romero at the defense table and a liberal, individual-rights judge on the bench, the outcome on this proceeding was less certain.

The bailiff announced the case and asked both counsel if they were ready to proceed. Both indicated that they were.

The prosecutor began by stating the charges against Damien Price, drug trafficking, unlawful possession of a controlled substance and resisting arrest.

As soon as the words were out of her mouth, Romero rose from her chair, "Objection!"

"On what grounds Ms. Romero?"

"Evidence against my client was obtained as the result of an illegal search and seizure."

"That's not true!" the prosecutor bellowed. "The search of the premises was conducted only after a valid search warrant had been issued by Judge Durbin."

"We're not questioning the search inside the home," Romero shot back. "We're questioning the search prior to entry into the home."

Judge Bush heaved a big sigh. He could tell it was going to be a long day.

The prosecutor requested that the officer in charge be allowed to testify and the judge granted her request with no objection from Romero.

Sergeant Winkler was called to the stand and sworn in.

For the next half hour, the prosecutor quizzed Winkler about the events of that morning which led to the arrest of Damien Price.

When she was finished the judge turned to Romero. "Your witness."

"Sergeant Winkler, what exactly led your task force to believe that there was illegal drug activity in that neighborhood?"

"Phone tips from neighbors that there were a lot of strange people coming and going late at night and in the wee hours of the morning, warning people to 'mind their own business'."

"Is there a curfew in that neighborhood?"

"Not that I'm aware of."

"So coming and going from a house, in itself, regardless of the time of day is not a crime?"

"I suppose not."

"Do you know everyone who lives in your neighborhood?"

"No, not everyone."

"Does being a stranger make one a drug dealer?"

"Of course not."

"Let's get back to these 'tips'. Did anyone actually see an exchange of controlled substances?"

"Not that I'm aware of."

"Any reports of violence, gunfire?"

"No."

"And yet, with this scant information, you felt compelled to investigate further?"

"Certainly. Many of our drug busts have come from law-abiding homeowners wanting to rid their communities of illegal activity."

"According to your testimony, you turned your canine friend, Buster, loose to roam through the neighborhood. What exactly was the purpose of that?"

"We suspected which residence was the drug house, but we wanted Buster to determine that on his own."

"So he sniffed more than one house?"

"Yes."

"What exactly was he doing?"

"Buster is trained to detect all kinds of drugs and he was search -----."

Winkler stopped in mid-sentence.

"What were you going to say, Sergeant? That Buster was searching for the odor of drugs?"

Winkler didn't answer.

Romero had him by the balls just as surely as Buster had mine.

I saw the prosecutor slump down in her chair.

Romero continued, "Sergeant, you're a veteran officer. What's required before a judge will issue a search warrant?"

"Probable cause."

"Exactly, and I believe that the Fourth Amendment states that the probable cause should be supported by an oath describing the place to be searched, and the persons or things to be seized.

"Actually, Buster searched not only Damien Price's home, but nearly every home on that block.

"Did you obtain a warrant authorizing Buster's search?"

"No."

"If you had asked a judge to issue such a warrant based on the comings and goings of individuals late at night, do you think that would have passed muster as probable cause?"

Winkler didn't answer.

"Sergeant, wasn't the warrant to search Damien Price's home based on Buster's detection of a controlled substance?"

"Yes."

"And without Buster's search, you actually had no probable cause to enter Damian Price's home."

"Yes."

Romero turned to the judge.

"Your honor, if I might, I would like to quote some case law that bears on this proceeding."

The judge nodded.

"Brenniger V. U.S. states that, *"Uncontrolled search and seizure is one of the first and most effective weapons in the arsenal of every arbitrary government."*

"That's why we have the Fourth Amendment.

"In Terry V. Ohio, *"The point of the Fourth Amendment, which often is not grasped by zealous officers, is not that it denies law enforcement the support of the usual inferences which reasonable men draw from evidence. Its' protection consists in requiring that those inferences be drawn by a neutral and detached magistrate instead of being judged by the officer engaged in the often competitive enterprise of ferreting out crime."*

"Your Honor, I submit that based on the testimony of the arresting officer, it is clear that the evidence obtained against my client was the result of an illegal search and seizure and a violation of my client's Fourth Amendment rights.

"We request that the charges be dismissed."

You could have heard a pin drop in the courtroom.

For what seemed an eternity, the judge sat there with his eyes closed.

At last he raised his gavel and pronounced, "Case dismissed! Mr. Price, you are free to go."

The courtroom erupted in pandemonium.

News reporters dialed cell phones calling in their stories and TV anchors jockeyed for the best position to interview anyone connected with the trial.

Suzanne Romero refused to comment as was her custom and the prosecutor was none to eager to make a statement for obvious reasons.

In the confusion, Ox and I slipped out the back door.

Ox was the first to speak, "Wow! That gal is something else!"

"Yep, we just got our asses handed to us on a platter --- again!"

"I don't want to go to squad meeting tomorrow. There will be hell to pay."

"It won't be pretty, that's for sure."

Buster's heroics and the department's dream case had turned into a nightmare.

Ed Jacobs had been eating lunch and had flipped on the TV to get the weather when the news bulletin flashed across the screen.

Ed had been following the story and, like everyone else, had fallen in love with Buster.

Also, like everyone else, he was thrilled that a drug dealer had been put out of business.

As he watched the report of the aborted court proceeding he suddenly lost his appetite and pushed his sandwich aside.

He felt the rage begin to build in his chest as Damien Price waved and smiled at the cameras.

Another miscarriage of justice.

The difference now, was that instead of letting that rage and frustration fester in his bosom, he had a way to make everything right.

If poor, blind, Lady Justice couldn't keep the scales in balance, it was up to him to restore equilibrium.

The reporters had made it incredibly easy for him.

Cameras had panned the street where the bust had taken place and focused on the bashed-in front door of Price's house.

Ed knew where Damien Price would be sooner or later.

He slipped on one of his disguises and drove the old Toyota down Myrtle Street.

He wasn't the only looky-loo. A steady stream of cars crawled by the scene of the police department's latest boondoggle.

He found the alley that ran behind the house and intersected with the driveway to the basement garage.

He noticed that there were no streetlights to illuminate the alley and later the area would be shrouded in darkness.

This was the spot.

Ed dressed in black including a black stocking cap that he pulled low on his head.

He blackened his face with grease paint. In the shadows at the back of the house, he would be invisible.

Both of his previous kills had been with rifles at long range. This one would be different.

He retrieved the .22 caliber pistol from his rented storage locker and checked his load.

He was ready.

Being early November, it was totally dark by six o'clock.

He drove through the neighborhood. It was mostly empty. The gawkers had gone home to dinner.

Price's house was dark. That was good. If he was already at home, he might not venture out again and the evening would be wasted.

Heck, he didn't even know if Price planned to return to his home. He might spend the night with friends celebrating his victory.

He had learned that patience was a virtue he must cultivate if he was to be successful.

He parked the Toyota several blocks away and made his way through the shadows to the alley and hid in some shrubbery at the back of the house.

There was a chill in the air and he shivered as he sat on the cold ground.

He could not see the faces of his previous two kills and as he waited, he wondered how he would feel staring into the eyes of his victim and seeing the fear and pain as the life drained from their bodies.

He had to keep reminding himself that this was no different than the deer he had killed.

Yes, it actually was different. The deer were innocent victims and these men were murderers, rapists and drug dealers.

He was lost in his thoughts when he heard the rumble of the Harley.

He flattened himself to the ground as the bike turned into the driveway and the headlight swept the back of the house.

He heard the garage door go up and the last cough of the big engine.

It was time.

He stepped into the doorway just as Price was removing his helmet.

Price froze, seeing the pistol pointing at his chest.

"Who --- who are you? What do you want?"

"Let's just say I'm here to balance the scales of justice."

Price made a grab for something in his saddlebag and Ed fired.

A look of disbelief came over Price's face as he watched the blood ooze from the hole in his chest.

"This is for all the kids you've hooked on pot and all the poor suckers that are high on your meth."

Ed fired again and Price slumped to the ground.

He waited for a moment and when Price didn't move, he looked into the saddlebag of the Harley.

Along with the .38 he had been reaching for, were the bottles of chemicals he needed to cook his next batch of meth.

"Not tonight," Ed said. "Not ever again."

Ed pulled the garage door closed and disappeared into the night.

At squad meeting the next morning, the captain shared the news that late last evening they had received a 911 call from a neighbor who had heard a shot fired at the home of Damien Price.

Responding officers found Price's body lying in a pool of blood and called for assistance. He was alive but barely breathing when the ambulance pulled into the emergency entrance at Truman Medical Center.

After several hours in surgery, the attending physician reported that Price had been very lucky and would survive.

The slugs that they removed from his chest were from a .22 caliber that had caused minimal internal trauma.

There was, however, significant blood loss and had the officers not responded quickly, he would have bled out.

After the meeting, the captain asked Ox and I to come to his office.

We were surprised to see that Judy DeMarco was already there.

Ox and I exchanged looks. It had not been a secret that Ox and Judy were dating, but both of us were wondering if we were about to be reprimanded.

Judy gave Ox a wink, so we both relaxed a bit.

The captain looked very serious.

"We've got to get a handle on this vigilante thing. The guy is making a mockery of the law.

"He got to Price last night, but he didn't finish the job. Our guess is that he will try to clean up his mess.

"We're betting he will come after Price and that's where the three of you come in."

I could tell that Judy was getting into it. "How can we help, Captain?"

"Price will be the bait and the three of you will be the trap.

"Officer DeMarco, who had extensive medical training while in the military, will go undercover as an attending nurse and Ox will be on the scene as a custodian."

"So what about me?" I asked.

The captain put on his best apologetic face. "Walt, if this wasn't so important, I wouldn't ask you to do this."

I didn't like where this was heading.

"With all the doctors, orderlies and nurses running around, we figured that we needed a non-threatening presence that wouldn't intimidate the vigilante and --- well --- there's hardly anything less intimidating than a candy striper."

I couldn't believe what I was hearing.

"WHY ME!"

Before the words were out of my mouth, I already knew the answer.

A year ago, the department had needed someone to go undercover in a tranny bar to smoke out some corrupt politicians and a couple of dirty cops.

Given my diminutive stature and the fact that I had much less body hair than anyone else in the squad, I was elected.

My 'Tina' persona was such a hit that I had somehow become the squads anointed drag queen.

"Walt, you do want to help us get this guy, don't you?"

What could I say?

He went to his closet and pulled out a red and white striped pinafore.

"I think this might be your size. Do you think Maggie could give us a hand again?"

Ox wouldn't look me in the eye and Judy had to bite her lip to keep a straight face.

Maggie, of course, was thrilled to help.

On my last foray into the world of cross-dressing, she had magically transformed me from a graying, sixty-six year old fart into something that was, at least, believable enough that I got propositioned at the bar.

During that makeover, I had absolutely no idea what was going on.

It was actually kind of scary that the transformation had now become familiar.

Feminine secrets like 'hook the bra in the front, then rotate to the back' and 'gather the leg of the pantyhose before inserting your foot' were second nature.

The make-up part was always the hardest.

No matter how close I shaved, Maggie had to spoon a lot of gunk on my face to cover the stubble.

I think I hated the eyeliner pencil and lash curler the most.

At the tranny bar, I had worn a wig with long brown tresses, but Maggie thought that something more 'perky' would be appropriate for a candy striper.

I donned a blond pageboy and when I looked in the mirror all I could see was Phyllis Diller on steroids.

When, at last, I was ready, the three of us gathered in the Critical Care Unit of the Truman Medical Center.

I was handed a badge that bore the name 'Fanny Merkle'.

Fabulous!

Ox was Lennie the custodian and Judy was Nurse Fremont.

I noticed right away that Judy filled out her nurse uniform a lot better that I filled out my candy striper outfit.

It clung to her curves and there was just enough room at the top to reveal a couple of inches of her ample cleavage.

I, on the other hand, looked like a gunnysack full of cats.

We were introduced to the head nurse in charge of the unit.

It was Nurse Ratchett all over again.

She had arms like a linebacker and the demeanor of a bulldog.

As I looked at the two nurses side-by-side, I couldn't help but wonder why, in all of my stays in medical facilities, I had always drawn a Nurse Ratchett and NEVER a Nurse Fremont.

"I don't know where you two came from," she snarled, "but when you're on my floor, you obey my rules! Got that!"

We got it.

"Fremont, check on Mrs. Snyder. She may need those damn bedsores dressed. Merkle, go with her in case she needs some help."

We went.

Mrs. Snyder had suffered a stroke and had been bedridden for months. Even though she had been turned regularly and massaged, she had developed bedsores.

Mrs. Snyder was not responsive and Judy motioned for me to help roll her on her side.

The bandages on the sores had come off revealing open wounds dripping pus and blood.

A stench that I had never encountered before hit me in the face.

I gagged and almost tossed my breakfast.

Judy grinned, "You've led a pretty sheltered life, haven't you?"

"If not having ever worked triage qualifies as 'sheltered', then yes."

After taking care of Mrs. Snyder, we checked in at the nurse's station.

Nurse Ratchett was ready with our next assignment.

"Mr. Goldblatt is ready for his sponge bath."

Goldblatt had been involved in a head-on collision resulting in a concussion and two broken arms.

He seemed to have recovered from the blow to the head, but his arms were both in casts and suspended from metal arms hanging over his bed.

He looked like a big stork preparing for flight.

We started at the top and were working our way down his body.

I noticed that he couldn't seem to keep his eyes off Judy's cleavage and whenever she would lean over to reach a difficult part, he would draw a sharp breath.

When we pulled back the sheets to wash his neither parts, we were both shocked to see that Mr. Goldblatt was sporting a woody as big as a Polish sausage.

He grinned at Judy, "How exactly do you pronounce your name? Is it Free - Mount?"

Judy rolled her eyes. "Look, Buster, if you think this bath is leading toward a 'happy ending', you've got another think coming. In fact, I think I'll just let Fanny here, finish you up."

He looked at me and I gave him a big wink.

By the time I got there, Mr. Woody had turned into Mr. Wimpy.

I suppose that it should have hurt my feelings, but I let it pass.

I finished with the libidinous Mr. Goldblatt and was heading down the hall when I heard, "Hey, Candy Gal. Can you get me a pudding cup? I really need a pudding cup."

I looked into the room where I had heard the voice.

A huge guy, probably at least three hundred pounds was sitting up in bed.

It was obvious that many a pudding cup had met its' demise at his hands.

"Please! I'm starving here."

I remembered my last visit to the hospital and how glad I was when Dad sneaked a breakfast biscuit into my room.

"I'll see what I can do."

I went to the nurse's station, but no one was around.

There was a small fridge. I opened it and saw cups of ice cream, jell-o and pudding cups.

He looked like a 'vanilla' guy, so I grabbed one and headed down the hall.

Just as I got to his door I heard, "Stop right there!"

A doctor came running up to me. "What do you think you're doing?"

"This guy wanted a pudding cup," I said, holding up the cup. "I was just trying to help."

"This man was admitted in a diabetic coma. We have him on a VERY strict food regimen. You could have ruined everything!"

"Sorry."

"If you intend to keep volunteering here, you will NEVER, and I mean NEVER, give anything to a patient without checking with a doctor or nurse. Do you understand?"

"I understand. I apologize."

I was afraid he was going to send me to the principal's office.

Having been thoroughly chastised, I decided to take a stroll by Price's room.

All three of us had been keeping an eye on it and now it was my turn.

Ed Jacobs was livid.

He had just read the morning headline in the *Star*,

"Vigilante Strikes Again, But Victim Survives!"

He realized that he had made his first mistake.

The old .22 just couldn't do enough damage.

He wouldn't make that same mistake again.

He knew he needed to finish the job, but he also knew the cops would be looking for him.

If he were going to succeed, he would just have to be smarter than them.

It was time to reach into his collection of disguises.

His first task would be to check out the situation and who better to roam the hospital halls unnoticed than the lowly janitor.

He spent his first afternoon locating Price's room. He was surprised that there were no uniformed officers on watch. He suspected that they had someone undercover.

He saw the usual doctors, nurses and orderlies as well as an older candy striper.

Another custodian named Lenny directed him to the laundry area where he found a doctor's smock that he carefully tucked away.

That night, he carefully crafted a badge bearing the Truman Hospital logo with his new name. He gathered the badge, a stethoscope, a clipboard and the smock and after carefully applying his makeup, he was ready to go.

He had watched who was coming and going in the halls and when everything was clear but the old candy striper, he decided to make his move.

The candy striper had entered Price's room and he followed close behind.

When she saw him, she dutifully stepped aside.

He approached the monitors and pretended to compare the current read-out with the clipboard he was carrying.

He turned, and with a serious look on his face, he addressed the woman.

"We have a problem. This man's electrolytes are spiking. I need to run some tests."

He looked at her name badge, "Uhhh, Fanny, could you please run to the nurse's station and ask them to bring a Henway Machine to the room? Stat!"

The woman looked at the doctor's name badge, "Sure, Dr. Guistizia. I'm on the way."

As soon as he was sure that the candy striper was gone, he withdrew a syringe from his smock and injected the contents into Price's angiocatheter.

He watched Price's body tense and then relax.

When he was sure that the drug had taken effect, he slipped out into the hall.

I had just reached the nurses station when a monitor started beeping.

A nurse looked at the monitor and immediately picked up a microphone.

"Code blue! Code blue!"

There was a flurry of activity as a doctor and several nurses pushing carts loaded with all kinds of stuff rushed down the hall.

To my horror, I saw them enter Price's room.

Ox and Judy met me in the hall outside his door.

I relayed what had just transpired.

"It looked like everything was fine when the doctor sent me to ask for a Henway Machine."

I saw the look on Judy's face. "Henway! You've got to be kidding me!"

"What? What's a Henway?"

She just shook her head. "About three pounds."

I looked at Ox, "Do you have any idea what she's talking about?"

Ox shrugged his shoulders.

"Henway!" she said again. "Don't you get it? What's a hen weigh? About three pounds!"

Then I got it. I'd been duped.

"At least the guy's got a sense of humor," Ox said.

At that moment the doctor and nurses came out of the room shaking their heads.

"We couldn't save him."

"What killed him?" Judy asked.

"We won't know until we do an autopsy, but my guess is that something was injected into his angiocatheter. How could this have happened?"

I relayed my story for a second time.

"I wasn't about to argue with another doctor. I had just got my ass eaten out by one."

"Did you see the doctor's name?"

"Yes, it was a weird one --- Giustizia, or something like that."

The doctor thought for a minute, "We don't have anyone on staff by that name."

A nurse standing close by spoke up. "Giustizia! That's the Italian word for 'justice'."

I wasn't sure how we were going to explain this to the captain.

CHAPTER 7

The press had a field day with our latest blunder.

The department was already reeling from the latest blow to its' creditability delivered at the hand of Suzanne Romero.

The fact that we had let the vigilante whack the same guy twice only added fuel to the fire.

Headlines screamed, *"VIGILANTE CLEANING UP DEPARTMENT'S MESS!"*

Every politician and pundit put in their two cents worth and every newscast had interviews with citizens on the street.

Advocates decried the liberal laws that seemed to give more protection to the criminals than the victims.

"In the United States today, where lawyers have tied the hands of law enforcement personnel to the point of police being rendered completely impotent, we see nothing wrong with an individual taking it upon themselves to stop crimes where they may be happening. This is not revenge. This is not criminal. This is right."

Victims and Citizens Against Crime spoke out boldly. *"People think a victim's nightmare ends when the attack is over. Not so. The nightmare is only beginning. For some, the shock and pain of what they now face at the hands of our criminal justice system can be as painful as the shock of being mugged, raped or having a loved one murdered.*

"Victims feel disenfranchised, isolated and even treated like criminals.

"They may suffer untold emotional grief, financial hardship and public humiliation, only to watch the offender become the center of attention in a legal system that goes to great lengths to protect the rights of the criminal. It is time to balance the scales and make the system more sensitive to the rights and needs of the victim."

Detractors screamed 'MURDER' and said that the vigilante was even worse than the offenders he was killing.

"Vigilante justice has been used to justify some of the vilest forms of violence in the history of this country. Many people have a view of what justice is and get bent out of shape if that view is not what is dealt. The only way to have a civil society is to follow the law and if we don't like it, work to change it. Otherwise, we are all subject to the punishment of what some other person views as justice."

Whoever it is that keeps track of these things reported that the vigilante's supporters outnumbered his detractors by a three to one margin.

Another byproduct of the vigilante's work was a groundswell movement against crime throughout the city.

Retailers and pawnshops reported a significant jump in the sale of firearms and 'concealed carry' classes were filled to capacity.

We also noticed a trend of a different nature.

Prior to the emergence of the vigilante, the majority of our emergency calls involved taking the statements of victims who had been robbed, mugged or raped.

As the days rolled by, more and more of these calls found perps being held at gunpoint or laying in a pool of blood.

Ox and I were patrolling midtown when a call came through.

"Car 54, what's your twenty?"

"Thirty-fourth and Broadway."

"Proceed to Westport Road and Pennsylvania. We have a report of shots fired."

When we arrived, a crowd had gathered around a red Ford Fairlane in the lot of a convenience store.

A middle-aged man was behind the wheel and a woman of the same age sat in the passenger seat.

A man in his mid-twenties with long, dirty dreadlocks and a face full of studs was prostrate on the ground.

The driver held up a snub nosed .38 by one finger. "Here, Officer. I figure you'll be wanting this."

"What happened here?" Ox asked, relieving the driver of his gun.

"We just stopped here to pick up some things," he said, pointing to a bag in the back seat, "and this guy approached our car and started waving a gun and telling us to get out of the car.

"So I just popped open my console where I keep the .38 and shot him. I figured it was either him or us."

"I don't see a gun," Ox said, looking around.

"It's under the body," an onlooker offered. "He fell on it."

"Did you see what happened?" I asked.

"Sure did. It was just like this fellow said. I saw it all."

Ox rolled the body and found a 9mm Glock.

So there it was --- self-defense pure and simple.

That evening, when I got to the apartment, my old friend, Professor Skinner, was just returning from his afternoon constitutional.

He noticed that I was a bit wrung out.

"Bad day, Walt?"

I told him about the shooting of the carjacker.

"Bernhard Goetz"

The name sounded familiar, but I couldn't place it.

"Who is Bernhard Goetz and what does he have to do with anything?"

"Bernhard Goetz was the Subway Vigilante.

"During the eighties, crime was rampant in New York.

"Goetz was riding the subway when he was accosted by four young punks who tried to mug him.

"He pulled a gun and shot all four.

"He was charged with attempted murder, assault, reckless endangerment and several firearms offenses.

"The subsequent trial initiated the first real nationwide debate on vigilantism."

"So what happened?"

"Much the same thing that is happening in our fair city. Public sentiment overwhelmingly supported Goetz.

"The jury included six people who had been mugging victims, consequently Goetz was found not guilty on all charges except illegal possession of a firearm. He served two-thirds of a one year sentence."

"And that applies to us how?"

"Goetz became a cultural hero. People realized they didn't have to be victims.

"They armed themselves and fought back. In the years following the subway shooting, New York went from being one of the most dangerous cities with a population over 100,000 to one of the safest.

"Criminals backed off not knowing if their next victim would be packing heat."

"So you're all for this vigilante thing?"

"I didn't say that.

"It's one thing for an individual to defend himself when being attacked. It's quite another when a man assumes the role of judge, jury and executioner.

"If everyone operated on that premise, we would be right back to Dodge City, Kansas in the early eighteen hundreds. The biggest, baddest guy with the biggest gun was the law.

"I hope we've evolved beyond that."

I said 'good night' to the Professor and climbed the stairs.

Maggie met me at the door. "Hurry, you're on TV."

The featured story on the news was our carjacking gone bad.

The cameras had captured Ox and me cordoning off the crime scene and taking statements from witnesses.

A reporter had approached me, but as instructed by the captain, all I could say was 'no comment'.

Realizing that they weren't going to get a sound bite from the cops, the reporter began interviewing onlookers.

Public sentiment was most definitely on the side of the intended victim.

Some of those interviewed waxed philosophical.

"A gun in the hand is better than a cop on the phone."

Maggie giggled and punched me in the arm.

Others were more serious.

"An armed man is a citizen. An unarmed man is a victim."

Our city was in a period of transition due to the actions of this vigilante and as far as I could see, there was no end in sight.

As wire services picked up the stories of the vigilante killings and the groundswell of citizens defending themselves against crime, Kansas City became a focal point in the ongoing national debate pitting gun control advocates against those championing the Second Amendment.

The first to hit town was the National Rifle Association, the foremost advocate of the right of the average citizen to bear arms.

Members of the Brady Center who were leading the battle for federal gun control laws soon followed them.

Local TV stations were quick to air interviews with members of both groups.

The NRA argued that the Second Amendment of the Constitution guarantees individuals the right to own and carry guns. They also argued that if law-abiding citizens have guns, they are safer from criminals, bringing crime rates down.

The Brady Center countered with statistics from *The New England Journal of Medicine*, stating that "*keeping a gun in the home makes it 2.7 times more likely that someone will be a victim of homicide in the home (in almost all cases the victim is either related to or intimately acquainted with the murderer) and 4.8 times more likely that someone will commit suicide, and that research has shown that a gun kept in the home is 43 times more likely to kill a member of the household, or friend, than an intruder."*

In spite of all the statistics quoted by the Brady Center, it seemed that Kansas Citians wanted no part in the government meddling with their right to pack a six-gun.

One of the more popular propaganda tools of the NRA was 'The Armed Citizen'.

It was a feature in their quarterly magazine and a fixture on their website where they related stories from all across the United States of ordinary citizens foiling crime and repelling attackers with everything from hatpins to twelve gauge shotguns.

Naturally, our local heroes were interviewed and became instant celebrities.

In their interviews they quoted timeworn slogans like, 'if guns are outlawed, only outlaws will have guns'.

When confronted with the Brady Center statistics, they countered with, 'if guns cause crime, then pencils cause misspelled words'.

All of this, of course, was a nightmare for the Kansas City Police Department.

They were between a rock and a hard place.

The vigilante was, without question, breaking the law and there was no choice but to use all the resources of the department to bring him in.

The failure of the department to do so made them a laughing stock and it was obvious that the majority of citizens were hoping he wouldn't be caught.

While the last high-profile case had been Damien Price, it was quite apparent to investigators that the vigilante was hard at work.

Every week, police were summoned to some remote alley or warehouse where the body of a known felon was found shot to death.

The police tried to keep a lid on these executions, not wanting to fan the flames of support for the man who was methodically exterminating the vermin of Kansas City.

Ed Jacobs was amused by all of the hullabaloo he had caused.

He watched all of the interviews on TV, both those calling him a murderer as well as those labeling him a hero.

He took personal satisfaction in seeing the man on the street fighting back against the criminal element.

After the Damien Price execution, Ed realized that, so far, his war against crime had been reactive.

His retaliation had come against criminals that had slipped through the loopholes of the legal system.

He decided that it was now time to become proactive.

He remembered that in *Death Wish*, Paul Kersey had taken a similar route.

In order to lure the bad guys into the open, he had used himself as bait, flashing wads of cash and carrying expensive cameras in dangerous neighborhoods.

The plan had certainly worked, but Kersey had gotten himself shot and stabbed for his trouble.

Ed wanted no part of that.

So the question was how to gain access to information about the scum terrorizing the streets without exposing himself to danger.

He reasoned that if one wanted to know what was happening on the streets, one should listen to the people on the streets.

He could think of no better place to rub elbows with the street people than at the local soup kitchens.

He did some research and decided that the best place to go was the Salvation Army.

Not only did they have a soup kitchen that provided hot meals every day, they also had a temporary shelter for the homeless and a battered women program.

The Army was always looking for volunteers and soon, Ed Jacobs was a regular fixture on the serving line of the soup kitchen, always watching, always listening.

He was perfectly safe and more important, who would ever suspect that the retired senior, ladling soup into the bowls of the homeless, was the notorious vigilante.

CHAPTER 8

While most of us in the squad were pre-occupied with the vigilante case, there was one among us whose thoughts were drawn in another direction.

Saying that Ox was 'smitten' was like calling the Grand Canyon a 'ditch'.

The guy was head over heels.

Since our night at the spook house, Ox and Judy had been out to supper several times and seen a couple of movies.

Each morning, when I quizzed him about how things were going, I always got the stock answer, "Fine --- just fine. We're --- uhhh --- taking it slow."

Then, one evening, Maggie and I were watching a movie on the tube when we heard a knock.

I opened the door to find my old friend standing there, white as a ghost, with a pathetic look on his face.

"Ox, what's wrong? Are you OK?"

He nodded his head 'yes' and then he shook his head 'no'.

"Get in here and tell me what's going on. Have you had an accident?"

"Not yet."

When we were seated, I patted him on the shoulder, "Ok, what's on your mind. I can tell this isn't just a social call."

He wrung his hands, "It's Judy."

"What! Is she OK? Did you guys break up?"

"No, no, nothing like that."

"Then what?"

He looked sheepish. "Tomorrow night will be our sixth date."

"That's wonderful!" Maggie exclaimed. "Where are the two of you going?"

"Well, that's just it --- we're not going anywhere. She's invited me to her apartment. She's going to cook dinner for us."

"So what's the problem?" I asked. "Are you afraid she's a lousy cook?"

"No --- no --- it's not that. It's ----."

"Ahhh, yes," Maggie said. "I think I know what you're problem is --- sixth date --- alone together in her apartment --- you're thinking maybe ---."

"Yeah, that's what I was thinking and I'm scared to death."

I was totally out of the loop. "Would somebody please tell me what's going on?"

"Oh, Walt, you're so dense," Maggie said, punching me in the arm. "Intimacy! Does that ring a bell?"

"Ohhhhh, that! With a gal like Judy I can see how that would make you nervous."

"WALT!" I got another whack on the shoulder.

Just then, there was another knock on the door.

I opened it and Dad and Jerry barged in.

"We saw Ox coming up the stairs and thought maybe something had broken in the vigilante case. What's up?"

"No," Maggie said, taking Dad by the arm and leading him to the door. "Nothing like that. He just dropped by to visit."

"Visit? You goobers see each other all day every day and you have to visit in the evening too?"

Maggie was insistent. "He just had something personal that he wanted to discuss."

That's when I made my first mistake.

"You know, given Dad's reputation as a ladies man, he might just be the perfect person to give Ox some advice."

Maggie gave me 'the look' and for a minute I thought she was going to pop a blood vessel in her forehead.

"Maybe Ox isn't comfortable discussing ---"

Dad cut her off, "Hey, if this has anything to do with a dame, I'm your man."

Then I made my second mistake; I put Ox on the spot.

"How about it, Buddy. Do you think Dad might be able to help?"

"Well --- gee --- I don't know."

By this time Maggie was livid. "Walt, remember what Ox thought might happen tomorrow night? Well you won't have to worry about that around here for quite awhile!"

"Oh, crap!"

Dad saw his opening. "I think I get your drift. You're hoping maybe the little lady is ready for some hanky-panky and you need some advice."

Ox shrugged his shoulders.

"Signals! You gotta look for the signals. When a gal's ready, she'll let you know, but you gotta know what you're looking for. Sometimes they're easy to spot. Other times they're more subtle."

Up to this point, Jerry had been quiet, but with Dad's lead in, he couldn't resist.

"Yeah, I knew a guy who took his girl out for dinner and after they had finished, he asked her what she'd like to do next.

"Her reply was, 'I wanna get weighed.'

"He thought that was a bit strange, but he wanted to make her happy so he stopped by a pharmacy that had a scale.

"When he dropped her off at her house, her mom asked how the date went and she replied, "Wousey!"

Ox looked perplexed, Maggie rolled her eyes and Dad roared out loud.

"Signals! See what I mean?"

It was apparent that Ox did not.

Dad wasn't finished. "Do you have protection, son?"

Ox was even more confused. "From what?"

"Condoms, rubbers, you know, safe sex and all that."

Now it was Ox's turn to get red.

Jerry was ready for his next salvo.

"Did you hear about the guy who went to the drug store for a package of condoms?

"The cashier rang them up and said, "That will be $5.00 with the tax.

"TACKS!" the guy shouted. "I thought that you rolled them on!"

That was the last straw for Maggie. "Out! Both of you out right now!"

Dad and Jerry saw the fire in her eyes and figured it was time for a hasty retreat.

As Dad was ushered out, he pumped his fist in a suggestive manner and said, "Go get 'em, boy!"

When they were gone, Maggie put her arm around Ox's shoulders. "I'm so sorry. They mean well."

"I know," he replied.

"You just be yourself tomorrow night.

"You're a great guy and Judy's a great gal.

"If it's meant to happen, it will happen and you'll know exactly what to do."

"Thank you, Maggie. I really appreciate it," he said, giving her a hug.

"Well, I'd better be going. See you tomorrow, Walt."

"Yeah, see ya."

When Ox had gone, Maggie gave me another 'look'.

"You're such a schmuck!"

Since Maggie had left little doubt that Mr. Winkie had no chance of becoming Mr. Happy tonight, I decided to flip on the TV and catch the late news.

The set came to life just in time to see 'BREAKING NEWS' flash across the screen.

An 'on the spot' reporter stood in the chill night air in front of a house on East 60th Street.

The flashing lights of half dozen police cruisers illuminated the front lawn.

The camera panned to the door of the home where cops were leading a man in cuffs to a waiting cruiser.

As he passed the reporter, the camera picked up his words, "I'm sorry! I'm so sorry!"

As the cruiser pulled away, the camera focused on the reporter.

"Tragedy has struck tonight in this east side neighborhood.

"Elvin Daniels, hearing his dog barking and a commotion in his back yard, went to the door armed with a handgun he had recently purchased.

"He saw a hooded figure running across his lawn carrying a shiny object in his hand.

"Daniels, fearing that the object was a gun, fired at the figure, striking him in the torso.

"The victim turned out to be the sixteen year old son of Danicl's next door neighbor and the shiny object was the student's Ipad.

"The victim died on the way to Truman Medical Center."

I sat in stunned silence.

It was bound to happen sooner or later.

Everyone suspected that it was just a matter of time until some trigger-happy citizen, riding the wave of mania that was sweeping our city, blew away an innocent victim.

I doubted that the NRA would be publishing this story in the 'Armed Citizen' column of their next magazine.

Gun advocates loved to use the quote, '64,999,987 firearm owners killed no one yesterday'.

They wouldn't be able to say that tomorrow morning.

Sunday mornings are usually pleasant in the Williams' home.

Maggie and I fix a big breakfast and over our second and third cup of coffee, read the paper, which on Sunday, is huge.

With things ending as they did the night before, I wasn't sure how this Sunday would turn out.

I figured I should try to make amends for my dimwittedness, so I started the day with an apology.

"Sorry about last night. I guess I wasn't real sensitive to Ox's needs and what you were trying to do."

Thankfully, Maggie is not one to carry a grudge.

Sensing my contrite spirit, she gave me a big hug and kiss.

"You're still a schmuck, but I love you anyway."

I brightened up immediately. "Really, does that mean ---?"

"Don't press your luck, Buddy!"

The paper that day had, of course, printed the story of the previous night's tragedy, but on the brighter side, with Thanksgiving only a few weeks away, there were numerous articles focusing on that special holiday.

Naturally, that brought up the topic of how we planned to spend our first Thanksgiving as a married couple.

Last year before we were married, Maggie and I decided that for the first time in our lives, we wanted to host a traditional Thanksgiving feast for all our close friends and family.

Given the fact that neither Maggie nor I knew squat about cooking, our feast turned out to be anything but traditional.

We were to fix the turkey, dressing, potatoes and gravy and everyone else was to pitch in with a dish of their choice.

The spread that eventually graced our table was a testament to the inadequacy of our culinary skills.

Without going into the gory details, we wound up with Mexicali turkey, crab-paste dressing and Aunt Jemima gravy.

This all went well with Bernice's hockey puck rolls that had been in her freezer since the Reagan administration.

The crowning glory was Willie's chitlins, the significance of which was somehow lost on the table full of old white folks.

Everyone else brought pumpkin pies and we wound up with enough pumpkin to feed the Mormon Tabernacle choir.

While the food left something to be desired, the fellowship was great.

But when it was all over, we vowed never to do it again.

I could see the wheels turning in Maggie's head.

"Walt, we have so much to be thankful for. We have each other. We have this beautiful home. We have our health. We both have jobs that we love and we have wonderful friends."

I couldn't argue with any of that.

"Maybe this year," she continued, "we could do something for someone else."

"Exactly what do you have in mind?"

"I don't know. There's always a charity thing going on around the holidays. I'm sure we can find something."

"Maybe we can talk to Pastor Bob," I suggested. "His congregation is always involved in something worthwhile."

While I am a firm believer in a Higher Power, the church scene has never been my bag.

But if I ever were to join a congregation, it would be Pastor Bob's.

I like him because he's not one of those 'holier-than-thou' kind of guys. He's down to earth and believes the message of the church should be how to live a better life and love one another by offering a helping hand.

On more than one occasion, when the burdens of my personal and professional life seemed more than I could bear, his counsel helped pull me through.

"That's a great idea," Maggie exclaimed. Then looking at her watch, "It's eleven thirty. Maybe if we hurry, we can catch him right after his services."

We pulled up in front of the Community Christian Church at twelve fifteen and Pastor Bob was just shaking hands with the last of his parishioners.

He smiled when he saw us approaching.

"I appreciate your attendance this morning, but for future reference, the service starts at eleven."

I gave him my best 'chastised' look. "Sorry about that."

"Not a problem. The topic of today's sermon was, 'In as much as ye give unto the least of these, my brethren, ye give unto me.'

"Seeing as how you're already a public servant, you probably didn't need that anyway."

I would have been offended, but he ended his barb with a wink and a smile.

"Actually, that's exactly why we wanted to talk to you."

After we shared our aspirations to Thanksgiving benevolence, he thought for a minute.

"So you're really serious about helping the less fortunate?"

"You bet. What do you have in mind?"

He looked at his watch. "Do you have any plans for the next couple of hours?"

I looked at Maggie and she shook her head.

"Good. Let me lock up the church and you can follow me in your car."

We followed Pastor Bob down Linwood Boulevard and parked in front of a big brick building with a sign over the door, 'Salvation Army'.

I had driven by this place, but I had never actually been inside.

A huge hall was filled with folding tables and metal chairs and along one wall was a serving line.

Men and women in aprons were filling the plates of one of the most diverse groups of people I had ever seen.

"Welcome to the soup kitchen," Pastor Bob said.

"Who are all these people?" Maggie asked.

"Good question. These are the homeless of our fair city.

"We used to have two main groups.

"See the old lady with the shawl around her shoulders? She's been homeless for years. She's a regular and we see her every day. She used to be part of our largest group.

"See that old guy in the stocking cap? He's one of the homeless that we only see when the weather gets bitter cold or when he can't find enough to eat panhandling or rummaging through dumpsters."

I felt Maggie shiver by my side.

"You said that woman used to be your largest group. What's changed?"

"Over there," Bob said, pointing to a man and woman with two small children.

"That's the Porter family. Mr. Porter lost his job. They had a lovely home on Cherry Street just south of UMKC. When he couldn't find work, they eventually lost their home to foreclosure.

"They've been living in their car ever since. He's found a minimum wage job, but they just can't get enough saved for a deposit and first month's rent.

"That family represents the 'new poor' of Kansas City. More and more of what we used to call 'middle class' families are now in the ranks of the homeless. It's tragic."

"Cherry Street!" Maggie said. "I've shown that home. It's darling. How sad they must be --- and those poor children!"

"The kids are still in school. The Ecumenical Council of Churches, which my congregation is part of, helps sponsor a breakfast and lunch program for families like the Porters."

"How can we help?" we both said at the same time.

"Will a serving spoon fit in your hand?" the Pastor asked.

"Never know until we try," I replied.

"Then let me get you both an apron."

With aprons in place, Pastor Bob led us to the serving line.

"Ed, I'd like you to meet Walt and Maggie Williams. You're just the guy to break them in proper."

A fellow about my age stuck out his hand.

"Ed Jacobs. Welcome to the trenches."

"So what do I do?" I asked.

"Well, it's not too technical. Can you hit a bowl with a stream of warm liquid?"

"My wife says I can't," I quipped.

Ed laughed, "You're going to fit in just fine."

CHAPTER 9

Our afternoon on the serving line was rewarding.

Seeing the plight of the homeless reinforced our appreciation for the lifestyle we had been blessed with and our desire to give back in some small way.

We wasted no time in sharing our experience with our friends and family and after doing so, found them willing recruits.

Actually, they were all probably relieved knowing that they would be spared another meal of Aunt Jemima gravy.

I appreciated Dad's attitude when he said, "When you were growing up, I was on the road all the time and I didn't get to do that kind of stuff with you. It's good to have a second chance."

Bernice, as usual, was OK to do anything as long as Dad was there.

Jerry was his usual self.

"Hey, I can certainly identify with those people. When I was growing up my family was so poor that if I hadn't been born a boy, I'd have had nothing to play with at all! I'm in!"

I knew that Mary wouldn't be left out on a bet and I was pretty sure that if Ox and Judy hadn't made any plans they would participate, so when it was all said and done, there were ten new volunteers for the holidays.

We decided that we should get as much experience as possible before the big day, so we volunteered for the evening meals as often as we could and worked weekends as well.

Ed Jacobs sort of took us under his wing. He not only showed us the finer points of manning the server line, he introduced us to the other volunteers and many of the homeless patrons.

I was surprised to see several of my tenants from the Three Trails come through the line and I felt guilty knowing that they relied on free meals in order to pay the forty bucks a week to keep a roof over their heads.

I realized that I was like most people, living life with my head stuck in the sand.

On Monday morning, I was anxious to see Ox and find out how the date had gone.

When we met in the parking lot, I noticed right away that he was grinning like the Cheshire Cat.

"Well ---- ?"

"Well, what?"

"Come on! You know what. How was the date?"

"Wonderful! Judy is a fantastic cook! Her meatballs and spaghetti were out of this world."

"I'm sure she is, but it wasn't the *MEAT*-balls that I was inquiring about."

"Walt, really! A gentleman doesn't kiss and tell."

"Oh, for heaven's sake --- I don't want details --- just hit some high points."

"Let's just say that given Maggie's comments to you on Friday night, I probably came out better this weekend than you did."

He got that right.

I didn't press the issue.

In squad meeting, the captain was reviewing the tragic case involving the shooting of the sixteen year old kid.

I noticed that he kept looking at Ox who was just sitting there with that same silly grin spread across his face.

Finally, the captain said, "Officer Wilson, do you find the topic I'm discussing this morning amusing?"

"Uhhh --- no, Captain --- Sorry."

The fact that Ox and Judy were dating was common knowledge in the squad.

Dooley couldn't resist. "Captain, I think I might have the answer. I'm guessing that Ox finally dipped his wick."

Instantly, all eyes turned to Judy.

You could see the disgust on her face. "What? Are we in high school here? And Dooley, I wouldn't be mouthing off if I were you. The word on the street is that you don't have enough wick to dip. All hat and no cattle if you know what I mean."

Dooley shut his mouth and slumped down in his chair amid the hoots and jeers of the squad.

The captain restored order. "If we could please get back to the matter at hand. Officer Wilson, please try to focus.

"Yes, Sir."

Ox did his best to keep a straight face, but every few minutes I could see the smile creep back on his lips.

It was obvious that his thoughts were elsewhere.

In the days that followed, Ed and I became good friends standing side-by-side, spooning glop on people's plates.

One particular conversation revealed what a small world it really is.

"So Ed, I'm guessing you're retired now."

"Yep, about three years now. My wife and I had one year of retirement together before she passed."

"I'm sorry."

"Yeah, me too. I miss her a lot."

I couldn't imagine what my life would be without Maggie.

Ed took a long look at me.

"Something about you is really familiar. I feel like we've met before."

"You know, I've had the same feeling."

"You don't happen to have a sister, do you? I recently met a woman that has a remarkable family resemblance."

"No," I replied, "I'm an only child. Well, actually I have a half-brother that I've only met once, but that's another story.

"What did you do before you retired?"

"I was a builder. Jacobs Homes."

"No! Really? You were the guy who built Blue Parkway Hills?"

"You know that subdivision?"

"Heck, yes! I was a Realtor for thirty years. Small world! I worked here in the city, but I certainly knew about Parkway Hills. That was a bold move, buying that land before the road was in."

"Yeah, it worked out pretty well. I was lucky. I got out just before the real estate bubble burst."

"Maybe that's where we've seen one another," I said. "Over the years, we've no doubt attended some of the same realtor functions."

"I'll bet you're right."

"So what keeps you busy these days?"

"Not a whole lot. After my wife died, I just kind of hung around the house and watched a lot of TV. I could see my health deteriorating so I decided to do something about it.

"I joined the YMCA and I work out there a few times a week and I'm attending a karate class for old farts. I've actually got a yellow belt."

"Is that good?"

"Not really, but it keeps me off the street. And, of course, I come here a lot."

I did notice that Ed was pretty fit for a guy our age.

"I noticed you said, 'I was a realtor'. So you're retired too?"

"From real estate. Maggie is still with City Wide Realty and she loves it."

"So what occupies your time?"

"Actually, I'm a cop. About two years now."

Ed nearly dropped his serving spoon.

When he regained his composure, "I'm not trying to get personal, but how does a guy your age get to be a cop?"

"It's a long story."

"Hey, I've got all afternoon and I'm all ears."

So I spent the next hour telling him about getting started with the Civilian Police Patrol and with the help of my partner, Ox, a lot of good luck and the blessings of a Higher Power, I was eventually accepted as a regular officer.

He was fascinated by my story. It's not every day you meet a sixty-seven year old rookie cop.

"So this vigilante thing must be keeping you pretty busy," he said.

"You have no idea. I've actually seen the guy, at least the back of his head. My partner and I were at the spook house the night he whacked LeShawn Grimes."

I thought about telling Ed about the hospital incident, but that would have meant revealing that my alter-ego was a cross-dressing candy striper named Fanny Merkle.

I decided it was a bit too early in our relationship for that.

Ed Jacobs smiled.

"Small world, indeed!"

The big day finally arrived.

We were all up before dawn and were eager to get to the dining hall and do our part.

The logistics of what was about to happen were staggering.

Before it was all over, a hundred and thirty turkeys would be baked, twenty-two gallons of gravy would be made (with absolutely no Aunt Jemima flour) and fourteen hundred dinner rolls would be served to four hundred people in the dining room and to another nine hundred elderly and homebound folks that couldn't make it in.

All this would be done with over three hundred volunteers.

They had been doing this for years and everything ran like clockwork.

We each took our assigned places and when the doors opened at eleven o'clock and the hungry masses invaded the dining room, we were ready.

It was interesting to watch the faces of the people as they made their way down the line.

The majority were obviously grateful for what was being provided for them and they thanked each one of us profusely.

Others were withdrawn and sullen, probably cursing whatever forces in the universe had dealt them their current lot in life.

When the line had finally dwindled to a trickle and the fed were soaking up the last bit of warmth before going back out on the street to face another cold night, a familiar figure climbed up on a small stage in the back of the room.

My heart skipped a beat when I saw that it was Jerry, and someone had given him a microphone!

Jerry, as you might have surmised, fancied himself the next coming of Rodney Dangerfield.

He was a regular at amateur night at the local comedy club and was used to performing onstage, but sharing yucks with a crowd that had come there to laugh was a whole lot different than a room full of the homeless.

This was bound to be a tough crowd.

I held my breath as Jerry spoke.

"In my wildest imagination, I could never understand what it is like to be in your shoes.

"Whatever the circumstances that brought you to this point in your life, I applaud you for not giving up the fight.

"There is an old saying that if life gives you lemons, make lemonade.

"The other choice is to chew on the bitter rind and be a sourpuss.

"What I have discovered is that those who choose to make lemonade are generally a happier lot.

"One way to make that lemonade is to laugh -- to find the humor in your circumstances --- and there always is humor if you will look for it.

"By laughing in its' face, you take away its' power over you."

I couldn't believe what I was hearing. This wasn't the lame, goofy Jerry I was used to.

He continued, "So, if you're ready to poke some fun at whatever it was that brought you here today, so am I.

"The first thing I want to do is thank all the fine folks that made this wonderful meal possible today. Let's give them a hand."

Everybody clapped and cheered.

"It's certainly better than one Thanksgiving I remember as a kid. We were so poor that when the wolf came to the door, we killed it and ate it!"

You could have heard a pin drop in the room, then, suddenly, from the back of the room, some guy bellowed, "That's hilarious! I love this guy!"

The room filled with laughter.

"I knew a kid that was so poor all he had to wear as a boy were hand-me-downs. It was a shame because all he had was five older sisters."

More howls.

"Any of you ever spend the night on a park bench?"

Hands shot up all around the room.

"This ever happen to you? A woman sits down on a park bench. It's a sunny day so she decides to stretch out her legs on the seat and soak up some sun.

"After awhile a bum approaches her and says, 'Hi beautiful. How about the two of us getting together?' 'How dare you!' says the woman. 'I'm not one of your cheap pick-ups!'

" 'No?' replies the tramp. 'Then what are you doing in my bed?' "

That one brought down the room.

Jerry carried on for another fifteen minutes and when he was through, left the stage to thunderous applause.

Maybe laughter is the best medicine.

Maggie grabbed my arm and we pushed through the crowd toward the table where the Porter family was seated.

She waved to a man that had been standing by the door and he joined us at the Porter's table.

"Mr. and Mrs. Porter, I'd like you to meet Mr. Glover. He's a client of mine.

"Actually, he's an investor and I showed him a beautiful home on Cherry Street.   "He fell in love with it and we closed just yesterday. He particularly liked it because of the way the previous owner had cared for it.

"Now he's looking for a tenant that will take care of it for him.

"I don't suppose you'd know of anyone looking for a nice place to live?"

The Porter's looked at one another. "Cherry Street? Our Cherry Street?"

Maggie nodded.

"But we don't have enough money for the rent and deposit."

Then Glover spoke. "You know, if I could find the right family, I might just waive that deposit."

Tears streamed down the Porter's faces.

The little girl looked questioningly at her mother. "Mommy, does that mean we can go home?"

"Yes, Dear. Now we can all go home."

I don't think I ever loved Maggie more than I did at that moment.

Thanks to my sweetie, the Porter family had something special to be thankful for that day.

The crowd started to thin and the massive job of clean up began.

Mary was pushing a big plastic trashcan on wheels, picking up the paper plates that people had left behind.

A couple of surly-looking characters were still at the table when Mary approached.

One of the guys blew his nose on a napkin and pitched it on the floor right at Mary's feet.

Surprisingly, Mary's first response was polite.

"Sir, I believe you dropped your napkin."

I guess she was just filled with the good spirit of the day.

The guy gave her the stink-eye and shot back, "So? Pick it up yourself, granny!"

You could see that the good spirit had quickly vanished by the fire in Mary's eyes.

"First, douche-bag, you should be grateful you got a place to come in out of the cold and get a hot meal.

"Second, you should show some respect for the folks that fixed it for you.

"And third, I ain't your maid, so get your skinny white ass out of that chair and pick up that napkin!"

He got out of the chair all right, but it wasn't to pick up the napkin.

Instead, he pulled a knife from inside his jacket and moved toward Mary.

"Bitch! Somebody needs to teach you a lesson!"

I was watching the whole incident unfold and sensed it was not going to end well, but I was behind the serving counter.

I pushed serving bowls aside and started to climb over the table when I saw Ed come flying across the room.

With a kick that would have made Bruce Lee proud, he struck the guy's arm causing the knife to fly across the room.

He followed the kick with a chop to the adam's apple that brought the guy to his knees.

Mary, of course, felt compelled to get in her licks and she firmly planted her number nine into the guy's gonads.

Groaning in agony, he fell to the floor.

Ed was on top of him in an instant and had the guy's arms pinned behind his back when the cops came busting through the door.

I showed the officer my badge and in fifteen minutes they were ready to drag the guy away in cuffs.

Mary wasn't about to let that happen. "Hold on a minute. I ain't through with him yet."

The officer looked at me and I nodded.

Mary grabbed the guy by the arm. "Now you're gonna pick up that napkin, wise ass. Or maybe you want some more of this!" she said lifting her foot.

The guy dutifully picked up the offending napkin and pitched it in the trash.

"Now you can have him!" she said, giving him a shove.

After calm was restored, I walked over to where Ed had taken a seat.

"You handle yourself pretty well for an old guy. Looks like those karate classes are paying off."

"I'm not sure what came over me. I just reacted. My instructor will probably be impressed."

An idea had been forming in my head and suddenly I just blurted it out.

"Last week when we were talking about how I became a cop, I didn't tell you the whole story."

Ed was apprehensive. "Yeah, so?"

I proceeded to tell him about the formation of the City Retiree Action Patrol and that I was the guy in charge.

He interrupted me. "You are aware that the acronym for your program is C.R.A.P.?"

"Yes, thank you very much for noticing."

He did his best to stifle a laugh.

"My only other recruit in the program is a fellow by the name of Vince Spaulding. He was a high school coach and, like you, his wife passed away.

"He felt like he still had something to give, so he became part of the program and has been an outstanding officer.

"Shortly after the formation of the Patrol, we did some work for Dewey Coughlin, the owner of the BuyMart chain. He was so grateful that he volunteered to underwrite the expenses of the program.

"We haven't spoken to him for awhile, but if he is still willing and the captain OK's everything, would you be interested in applying for the City Retiree Action Patrol?

"I think you'd make a fine addition to our squad."

Ed sat in stunned silence.

"Wow! That's a lot to consider!

"Let me think about it and I'll let you know."

I hadn't planned to invite Ed to join us, but somehow, it just seemed right.

CHAPTER 10

The winter sun had set by the time we had served and cleaned up after four hundred people.

We were all tired and Mary was still wired from her encounter with the litterbug.

I heard her grumbling in the backseat, "I should've whacked his nuts one more time before the cops took him. That boy needed a lesson."

We pulled up in front of the Three Trails and Maggie whispered, "Why don't you walk her to the door. She's had a rough day."

Reluctantly, I agreed, and we strolled up the sidewalk together.

When we reached her front door, we both saw it at the same time.

The frame was shattered and the door was ajar.

"DAMN!" she exclaimed. "We've been hit again --- and on Thanksgiving, too. What's the matter with people?"

I told her to wait outside and I cautiously searched the apartment, but the intruder was long gone.

As before, none of Mary's personal effects were missing, just the rent money.

The first time I hoped it was an isolated incident, but with this second intrusion I figured it was time to make a report.

I called it in and soon a cruiser pulled up in front of the hotel.

By this time, word had spread throughout the building that we had been hit again and rent had been taken.

As before, everyone had magically paid their rent on that very day.

The officers took the report and when we told them that this was the second break-in, they called the CSI unit to dust for prints.

When everyone had gone, poor Willie stood in front of the door shaking his head.

"Dey keep bustin' dis in, dere ain't gonna be nuthin' left to fix."

He did a quick patch job and we headed for home.

In spite of all the tribulations of the day, we still had a lot to be thankful for.

Ed Jacobs couldn't believe this incredible turn of events.

So far, everything he had done had gone exactly according to his well-laid plans.

He had rid the Kansas City streets of vicious predators and the police still didn't have a clue as to his identity.

He had volunteered at the Salvation Army to get leads on more scumbags who deserved his attention and it had worked wonderfully.

And now, providence had brought to the serving line, exactly the fellow who could take his campaign to the next level.

Wearing the badge would give him access and inside information on every creep that committed a crime.

He could keep tabs on the progress that the police were making in their investigation of the vigilante, and most important, who would ever guess that the vigilante himself was one of KC's finest.

There was no question about it.

He was ready to become a member of the City Retiree Action Patrol.

He smiled as he remembered the acronym.

When this adventure began, how could he have ever guessed that he would be involved with C.R.A.P.?

I was thrilled when Ed called and said he was ready to take the leap.

I cautioned him that it wasn't a done deal yet. I had to clear it with the captain and Dewey Coughlin.

That proved to be just a formality. Both Vince and I had been valuable additions to the department and if Coughlin was still willing to foot the bill, the captain was grateful for the extra manpower.

Coughlin was logging some great publicity each time Vince or I were involved in a big collar, so he was more than ready to add more accolades to his public image.

With all that out of the way, it was time for Ed to begin the application process.

He had to pass a written test, a physical and an oral review.

If he made it to that point, he would begin his physical training in hand-to-hand combat and qualify on the firing range.

He breezed through the physical and the written test without a problem.

On the day of his oral review board, the captain asked if I could attend and give Ed an endorsement.

As I looked back on my own oral review, I was amazed at the changes in attitude that had taken place in two short years.

At that time, no one believed that an old fart like me had any business being a rookie cop and I really didn't blame them.

I passed by the skin of my teeth, but only after I shot one of the beligerant captains with a taser.

Now, two years later, these same guys are asking my opinion about hiring another old geezer.

I felt proud and happy to share my experience with Ed at the Salvation Army and relate his heroics in saving Mary.

Ed's karate training made the PT class a breeze and everyone was amazed at his proficiency with a handgun.

He passed his first time on the firing range.

On the day he received his badge, Ed had a whole cheering section in the audience.

Maggie, Dad, Bernice, Jerry, Willie, The Professor and Mary were joined by at least a dozen other volunteers from the Salvation Army to wish him well in his new career.

Lady Justice just got a new recruit.

Ed Jacobs had just clocked out and was heading to his car when he saw a familiar face standing on the curb waiting for the Metro bus.

It was the jackass that had pulled the knife at the Thanksgiving dinner.

Ed had been keeping tabs on the guy and was disappointed to hear that he was going to be cut loose.

Since no one was actually injured in the altercation other than the perpetrator himself, and given the crowded conditions in the jail, the judge had sentenced him to time served and two hundred hours of community service.

Another travesty of justice.

Ed had seen the look in the soulless eyes of the sociopath as he wielded the knife, and he knew it was just a matter of time until he actually claimed a victim.

Ed waited patiently in his car until he saw the perp climb aboard the bus.

He pulled into the traffic lane and followed at a safe distance.

The perp exited the bus at Twelfth and Monroe and after pausing a moment under the glare of the streetlight, he made his way to the Monroe Bar and Grill.

Ed found a parking space on the street where he could watch the entrance.

Patience.

An hour later, the perp staggered onto the street. It was obvious that his goal had been to make up for the drinking time lost while in lock-up.

Ed watched him weave down the street and disappear into an alley.

He followed and found the guy with his pants unzipped taking a leak behind a dumpster.

After zipping up, he pulled a tissue from his pocket, blew his nose and tossed the tissue onto the pavement beside the dumpster.

Ed approached with his gun drawn.

"Looks like ten days in lock-up didn't teach you a lesson."

The guy squinted at Ed through bloodshot eyes.

"You a cop?"

"You got that right and you're under arrest for littering and urinating in a public place."

Ed pointed to the tissue.

"Now pick that up and put it in the dumpster."

"You gotta be kidding, man."

Ed waved his gun. "Do I look like I'm kidding?"

Ed watched as the guy dutifully deposited the offending tissue.

"You probably never watched Woodsy Owl when you were a kid, did you?"

The guy looked perplexed. "I don't know what you're talking about, man. You're crazy!"

"Woodsy Owl told us to 'Give a hoot --- Don't pollute'. Now look what you've gone and done," he said pointing to the steaming puddle of urine.

"Did you know that you can get the death penalty for littering and urinating in public?"

"That's crazy, man! There ain't no death penalty for that stuff!"

"There is today!" Ed said, pulling the trigger.

As the guys warm blood mingled with the steaming urine, Ed smiled.

"Every litter bit hurts."

The vigilante had struck again and this time, it hit close to home.

Ox and I were on patrol when a body was found in an alley on Twelfth Street.

We were dispatched to the scene to help cordon off the area and for crowd control.

I took a look at the body and immediately recognized the guy that had pulled a knife on Mary at the Salvation Army.

Ox recognized him too.

"Why do you suppose this jerk got the vigilante's attention? He was just a street punk."

"Well, we actually don't know it was the vigilante. He could've pissed someone off at the bar down the street."

"Didn't he just get released yesterday?"

"Yep, and that might have been what peaked the vigilante's interest if it was him --- time served and community service. Not exactly a stiff sentence for threatening someone's life."

After the crime scene guys finished their work and the body had been carted off to the morgue, Ox and I were ordered to help with a canvass of the neighborhood.

As usual, no one had seen or heard anything.

CHAPTER 11

The next morning, on my way out, Willie flagged me down.

"Mr. Walt, hold up a second."

"What's up, Willie?"

"It's Louie de Lip. He wants to talk wit' you."

Louie the Lip was a holdover from Willie's days as a street hustler. They had stayed in touch and on more than one occasion, Louie's proximity to Kansas City's underbelly had helped us solve some crimes.

In fact, it was Willie and Louie that had saved my sorry ass one night when Joey Piccolo, a street punk, had tried to bring my law enforcement career to a premature end.

I owed Louie and he knew it. I wondered if this was payback time.

"Any idea what he wants to chat about?"

"It's dem Ruskies. Dey back in Northeast.

"He says to meet him in de parkin' lot at Union Station. He be sittin' on de bench at de bus stop."

"Tell him that I'll swing by after squad meeting."

When squad meeting had concluded, the captain summoned Ox and me.

"Ed Jacobs' partner called in sick this morning. I'd like to have Ed ride with you. Maybe he can pick up some tips from the 'Dynamic Duo'."

"Sure, Captain, no problem."

As we pulled out of the parking garage, I told Ox about my conversation with Willie.

"Better head to Union Station, then," he replied.

We turned off Main Street onto Pershing Road and I saw Louie sitting on the bus bench.

Ox pulled up in front of the bench and Louie slipped into the backseat beside Ed.

"Hey, Louie," I said.

"Walt. Ox,"

Louie was one of those characters that once you see, you'll never forget.

They say some girls have 'Betty Davis eyes', well, Louie has 'Mick Jagger lips'.

He looked over at Ed. "Who's dis guy?"

"Ed Jacobs, meet Louie. Ed's a new recruit. He's with me. He's okay."

Ed stuck out his hand, but Louie just nodded. I guess you had to earn his trust.

"So what's up?"

"It's dem Ruskies. Dey tryin' to get back in Northeast.

"De I-talians and us, well, we got us an arrangement. Dey do dere stuff and we do our stuff and nobody gets hurt, but dese Ruskies, dey want ever'ting.

144

"Word on de street is dat de Ruskies is gonna start hittin' de I-talians. If dey do, dere's gonna be blood all over Northeast and none of us wants any part of dat."

"So how do we fit in?"

He turned to Ox. "Head north on Main an' I'll show ya."

Just before we got to the old Argosy Hotel, he said, "Pull to de curb."

The Argosy was another throwback to Kansas City's bawdy days of the thirties.

Once a fine hotel, it had deteriorated into a flophouse that made the Three Trails look like a Hilton.

"See dat SUV?" he asked, pointing to a black Caddie.

"Yes."

"Well, dat belongs to a Ruskie who's stayin' dere. Word is dat he's de guy what's gonna do de hit."

"So what do you want us to do?" I asked. "Do you expect us to tail him and take him down before he blows someone away?"

"Well, you de cops, ain't ya?"

We dropped Louie back at the bus stop and headed back to the precinct.

"Well that was pretty 'cloak and dagger'," Ed said. "Do you guys do that a lot? And what was that name that the captain called you?"

"You can call me Bond," I quipped. "James Bond."

We relayed our story to the captain.

"And exactly who told you all of this?"

Ox and I had already decided that we had to keep Louie out of the picture.

"It was an anonymous tip."

The captain looked skeptical. "Maybe we should see what Organized Crime has to say about all this."

He made a call and in a few minutes we were telling our story to an officer from the Organized Crime Unit.

"We've heard some scuttlebutt about that, but nothing solid. Are you sure this 'anonymous tip' is authentic?"

"It sure sounded like it."

"I'm short on manpower. If the captain can spare you, let's put a tail on the guy."

"Us?" I asked. "We don't exactly blend into the scenery in a squad cruiser."

"I've got something that will help."

He left the room and returned with a device about the size of a cell phone, and an IPad.

"GPS," he said. "Magnetic. Stick this thing under his wheel well and you can track him from several blocks away. He'll never know you're around."

After a quick lesson, we were on our way.

Ed secured the GPS in the Caddie's wheel well and we parked on Grand, a couple of blocks away.

After about an hour had elapsed, the green blob on the screen started moving.

"There he goes," Ox said. "Looks like he's heading north."

We followed at a safe distance and watched as the blob stopped in the nine hundred block of Troost.

"Benny 'The Butt!" Ox said.

"What?"

"The pawn shop. There's a pawnshop in that block owned by Benny 'The Butt' Buttafusco. I'll bet that's the target. We'd better hurry!"

Ox slammed the cruiser into gear and we sped to the pawnshop.

Sure enough, the SUV was parked in front of the shop.

Through the bars on the front windows, we could see a really big guy pointing a really big gun at another guy with a really big butt.

It wasn't hard to tell which one was Benny. It looked like every ounce of pasta that he had ever eaten had gone right to his ass. It looked like he had a pair of saddlebags strapped to each hip.

We slid to a stop and ran into the pawnshop with guns drawn.

The big guy, seeing that he was outnumbered three to one, surrendered his weapon.

We called for assistance and when everyone was gone but us, I whispered to Benny, "You can thank some of your 'bruddas' on the street for this."

He nodded and he understood.

The Russian's name was Vladimir Postnikoff.

The three of us, as arresting officers, were required to be at the preliminary hearing.

My heart sank when I saw Suzanne Romero at the defense table.

"*Not again!*" I thought.

She had made fools of us with the dog search and here she was again.

I was on the hot seat last time. It was Ox's turn.

The Prosecuting Attorney called him to the stand and asked him about the arrest.

He told how we followed Postnikoff and arrived at the pawnshop just in time to see him pointing a gun at Benny.

When it was Romero's turn, she wasted no time.

"Officer Wilson, tell us again why you followed the defendant."

"We received an anonymous tip."

We had decided that was our story and we were sticking with it.

"When did you first see Mr. Postnikoff?"

"At the pawn shop."

"So you didn't see him leave the Argosy Hotel?"

"No, Ma'am."

"If you didn't see him, then how could you have followed him?"

"We had one of those GPS tracking things. We put it under his car."

"And just where did you get the 'tracking thing'?"

"An officer from the Organized Crime Unit gave it to us."

"And did that officer obtain a warrant for the device?"

Ox looked at the Prosecutor and you could see the color drain from his face.

"I --- I don't know. I never saw one."

"According to your testimony, you said that you saw my client in the pawn shop with a gun. Is that correct?"

"Yes."

"Doesn't Mr. Buttafusco take guns on pawn?"

"I suppose so."

"Then how did you know that he wasn't just trying to pawn his gun?"

"Well, because of the tip."

"From an anonymous source?"

"Yes, Ma'am."

Romero turned to the judge.

"Your Honor, once again, the police department is running roughshod over our Fourth Amendment rights.

"It protects a citizen's persons, houses, papers, and effects, against unreasonable searches and seizures.

"A person's automobile is certainly part of a person's 'effects'.

"For years now, a warrant has been required for tapping phone lines and searching the interior of cars. The placement of a tracking device on an automobile is no different.

"Every person should have an expectation of privacy, subject to the issuance of a warrant.

"And, once again, a warrant can only be issued with probable cause.

"The officers involved did not know or even see who they were tracking and did so based on an anonymous tip.

"Your Honor, would you have found probable cause and issued a warrant based on that information?"

The judge didn't answer.

"Your Honor, I move that the charges against my client be dismissed as any evidence provided by the prosecution was obtained in violation of his Fourth Amendment rights."

The judge banged his gavel. "So ordered."

As Romero was turning away from the defense table, the Prosecutor grabbed her by the arm.

"If there's a gang war and a bloodbath in Northeast, it's on you!"

She pulled her arm away. "No, if there's a bloodbath, it's because you guys can't get your shit together.

"If Missouri ever turns into a police state because our constitutional rights have been taken away, then *that's* on me!"

She turned and stalked out of the courtroom.

Ed had been involved in the case from the beginning and, hard as he tried, he couldn't see how anyone could have done anything different than what was done.

Romero was right. No judge would have given them a warrant, but their actions had prevented, or at leased postponed, a street war.

He understood that our rights had to be protected, but he also knew that the protection sometimes lets criminals slip away.

That's why they needed him.

He dug through his disguises and found just what he was looking for.

No one would suspect that the old street bum looking for a warm place to spend the night was actually a cop --- no --- the vigilante.

He checked into the Argosy and hung out in the lobby until he saw the Russian park the SUV.

He followed him up the steps and as the Russian pushed open his door, Ed was right behind him.

Postnikoff was bigger, younger and stronger than Ed, so he wasted no time.

Before the Russian could regain his footing, Ed fired his silenced revolver and the Russian slumped to the floor.

This time it wasn't enough to just eliminate the threat. He needed to send a message as well.

He took a can of aerosol spray paint from his coat and went to work.

When he had finished, he looked at his handy work.

Perfect!

Quietly, he left the hotel by the back stairs and slipped out into the night.

Ox and I had just started our shift when we received the call that all units in the area were to respond to the Argosy Hotel.

A homicide detective had arrived just before us and was examining a body in an upstairs room.

When the call came in, we knew that the Argosy was where the Russian was staying, and it came as no surprise when we saw that the dead guy was him.

Ox pointed to the wall.

There, in bold, red letters, were the words, "NOT IN KC!" and under them was the letter 'V'.

"The vigilante!" Ox said. "He's sending a message to the Russians that it was him and not the Italians that had taken the guy out. How did he know?"

We interrogated the manager of the hotel and, of course, he had heard nothing.

We asked him if there had been any strangers hanging around the night before.

"Just an old street bum. He had panhandled enough dough to get off the street last night. Checked in about seven."

"I don't suppose you keep a record of who is here?"

The clerk looked offended. "We make them sign in."

"So did this guy sign in?"

"Sure did. Had kind of a funny name too. Said his name was Vincent Justice. Here look," he said, handing us the logbook.

We looked, but the log didn't say Vincent Justice. It said, "V. Justice".

I looked at Ox. I'm guessing that stands for 'vigilante justice.'

It was going to be another long day.

When I returned home that evening, Willie met me at the door.

"Louie says to tell you 'thanks'. You droppin' de word to Benny about de bruddas, kept things real cool. Now everting's copacetic."

I was thrilled that I could do my part to keep things on an even keel in the underworld.

CHAPTER 12

Maggie and I had just sat down to supper when the phone rang.

"Walt, this is Crenshaw."

I recognized the voice. "What's up, Officer?"

"I think maybe you should come over to the Three Trails. There's been a shooting. We've got a body."

My mind immediately went to Mary.

"Mary Murphy! Is she okay?"

"Actually, Walt, Mary was the shooter."

Maggie and I threw on our coats and headed out the door.

When we arrived at the Three Trails, cruisers with lights flashing had blocked the street and crime scene tape was strung around the hotel.

A body lay in a pool of blood at the end of the sidewalk and my old friend Mary was on the porch in handcuffs.

I looked for Crenshaw, but before I could find him, Detective Derek Blaylock waved me over.

"Blaylock! What are you doing here?"

Blaylock was one of the senior detectives in Homicide. We had worked together on several cases. He was a good cop and a friend.

"Direct orders from the Chief. When word came down that there had been a shooting at a building owned by a cop, the brass wanted to make sure everything was done by the book."

"Why is that so important?"

"It's about all this vigilante and armed citizen crap. It's bad enough when ordinary folks start blowing each other away, but when a cop is involved in any way, they want to cover their bases."

"So what happened?"

"Looks like the guy on the sidewalk, Mario Bondell, broke into Ms. Murphy's apartment and threatened her with a knife.

"She pulled a gun and he ran out the door. She followed him and shot him dead."

"So it's self defense. Why is Mary in handcuffs?"

"I'm afraid it's not that simple, Walt. Look where the body is laying."

"Yeah, so?"

"So the guy was fleeing. The immediate threat of bodily harm was gone. She chased the guy and gunned him down. I'm afraid that this is second degree murder --- at the least manslaughter."

"But it's Mary!"

"Exactly! And that's why the Chief wanted me here. With all the publicity going on with this armed citizen stuff, we can't just sweep something like this under a rug, especially since she's a close friend of a cop. The press would crucify us."

"Can I talk to her?"

"Not now. We're taking her downtown to central booking. After she's processed you can see her."

Just then an officer led my old friend, trussed in handcuffs, to a waiting cruiser.

For just a moment our eyes met and I could see the terror etched in her face.

In that instant, I wasn't a cop. I was just like a hundred other guys I had seen on TV as they watched a loved one being taken away, and I shouted, "Mary! Don't say a word to anyone! Not a word! I'll see you at the station."

Tears flooded my eyes as I saw Mary's face, pleading with me, as the cruiser pulled away.

I dropped Maggie off at our apartment and headed downtown.

On the way, I tried to wrap my head around what had just happened.

It was like a bad dream --- no, a nightmare, and the image of Mary's pleading face kept popping into my mind.

I parked and made my way to central booking and was surprised to see Captain Short there at this late hour.

When he saw me, he took my hand. "Walt, I'm so sorry about Mary."

"Captain, why are you here this late?"

"I wanted to see you in person --- to talk to you."

"Well I'm glad you're here. Maybe we can get this mess cleared up."

"That's why I needed to see you. I'm afraid we're not going to be able to make this go away."

I was stunned. "Why not? I don't understand."

"Walt, it all boils down to this --- the department has been taking it in the shorts from the press and the powers-that-be have decided it's time to take a stand against all this armed citizen crap.

"They've been looking for a solid case to prosecute as a warning to our citizen gunslingers and Mary's situation seems to fill the bill, especially since she works for a cop. The image they want to project is that the City is tough on crime --- no exceptions."

"So this came from the Chief?"

"No, Walt. Higher up the food chain than that. The department would never throw one of its own under the bus for publicity's sake."

"Who then? The Mayor?"

The Captain just shrugged his shoulders, but it was obvious that the answer was 'yes'.

"So this is all about politics? Mary's is being offered as the sacrificial lamb to polish the Mayor's public image?"

The Captain shrugged again. "I'm really sorry, Walt. I wish there was something I could do."

"Well, I have some vacation days coming. I'd really like to take some time off until this thing is settled."

"Take as much time as you need. Mary needs you."

The guy from booking stuck his head out of the door.

"Walt, we're through processing Mary. You can see her now if you want to."

I followed him to a holding cell and saw Mary sitting there on a cot with a glazed look in her eyes.

When she saw me, she rushed to the bars. "Oh, Mr. Walt. I knew you'd come. What's going to happen to me?"

"You haven't made any statements, have you?"

"No! You said not to."

"Good. You will be arraigned in the morning and then we'll get you out on bail."

"I gotta spend the night here?"

"I'm afraid so, but we'll get you out tomorrow."

"Mr. Walt, I'm scared --- more scared than I've ever been."

"I know, Mary. Try not to worry and try to get some sleep. We'll work through this together. I'll be with you every step of the way."

"Thank you, Mr. Walt."

As I drove home, my first reaction was sadness, seeing Mary like that.

Then, the more I thought about the situation, the madder I became.

From the moment the badge was pinned on my chest, I had been proud to be an ambassador for our City, but at that moment, all I was feeling was contempt.

After I joined the force, I came to realize that justice is like a big chess game, the criminals on the street versus the law.

Guys on the beat like Ox and me are merely pawns, manning the front lines, and, as in chess, it's sometimes good strategy to sacrifice a pawn for the greater good.

The Captains are the knights, doglegging through the red tape of the law, trying to make the best case against the perps.

The Chief is the castle, charged with bridging the gap between the working stiffs and City Hall.

The Prosecuting Attorneys are the bishops, seeing the law from every possible diagonal rather than straight on.

The Mayor is the queen, the most powerful piece on the board, with the ability to move in any direction that suits his fancy, and, of course, the queen must be protected at all costs.

The king is the citizen on the street and if all of the other pieces fail to do their jobs, it is the king that falls to the opposing forces.

In chess, it is the duty of every other piece to protect the king, but unfortunately, I had discovered that in real life, sometimes even the king is sacrificed to protect the interests of the queen.

In my two years on the force, I had seen hardened criminals walk free due to procedural errors, expediency or deals made to catch a bigger fish.

It was all part of the game.

But now, it was my good friend, Mary, the sweetest, most law-abiding citizen you would ever want to meet, that was being hung out to dry as an example in the City's 'get tough' policy.

The Mayor was using Mary to take the heat off of himself and I wasn't about to let that happen.

I flipped open my cell phone and dialed the home number of a lawyer friend of mine.

"Hi, this is Walt. I need a favor. You probably have a list of home or cell phone numbers for attorney's, don't you?"

In just a few minutes, I had the number I was looking for.

I dialed and the phone was answered on the third ring.

"Hello. Suzanne Romero here."

"Ms. Romero, so sorry to bother you at home. I'm Officer Walt Williams and I need your help!"

The courtroom was crowded as it always was when Suzanne Romero was at the defense table.

The bailiff called the court to order and Judge Warren Franklin took the bench.

The case was called and the judge asked for appearances.

"Bernard Larkin for the Commonwealth, Your Honor."

Everyone was surprised to see the District Attorney himself presiding over the trial and not one of his minions.

"Suzanne Romero for the defense."

"You may proceed, Mr. District Attorney."

"Case number 319455, the Commonwealth versus Mary Murphy on the charge of murder in the second degree."

"How does you client plead, Ms. Romero?"

"Not guilty, Your Honor."

"So noted. Is there a request for bail?"

"Yes, Your Honor. Ms. Murphy has no criminal record; she is gainfully employed and is not a flight risk. We ask that she be released on her own recognizance."

"Any objection, Mr. Prosecutor?"

"Yes, Your Honor. This is a felony murder charge. We would have no objection to bail in the amount of fifty thousand dollars."

"So ordered!" The judge banged his gavel and called for the next case.

The bailiff led Mary out of the courtroom and Suzanne motioned for me to meet them in a conference room.

When we were all together, Mary's first comment was, "Mr. Walt. I ain't got fifty thousand dollars. I barely got fifty dollars. Does that mean I gotta stay here?"

"No, Mary. I'll take care of that. You'll be out of here by noon."

I figured this was coming and I had made arrangements to use my apartment building to guarantee bail.

Suzanne Romero was all business.

"Mary, the District Attorney has offered us a deal."

"What kind of deal?"

"You are being charged with second degree murder. If you're convicted, you could get up to twenty years. At your age that would most likely be a life sentence.

"If you are willing to plead guilty to manslaughter, they will recommend five years. With good behavior you could be out in two."

"I'd have to go to jail for two years? For killing a guy that broke into my place and put a knife to my throat? That just ain't right!"

"No, it's not right, but that's the offer on the table."

Mary thought for a moment. "I'm just too damn old to be some prison dyke's bitch for two years."

Suzanne smiled, "Mary, you've been watching too much cable TV. Most likely we could get you in a minimum-security facility. Some of them are almost like a country club."

Mary looked at me. "What about the hotel. Who would run the hotel for you?"

"Let's not worry about that. Let's figure out what's best for you."

Mary thought some more. "I'm seventy-three. It don't matter whether it's two years or twenty. Either one would be a life sentence for me. I killed that guy fair and square and I ain't apologizing for it."

"Well, Suzanne," I said, "what are our chances? I've seen you let rapists and drug dealers walk out of here free men, can you do the same for Mary?"

"First, I took those cases because someone in your department screwed up and deprived the jerks of their civil rights.

"It's not about getting a criminal off the hook. It's about protecting our constitutional rights.

"If governments are not held accountable and made to obey the law, that affects every American citizen. Just ask someone in Iran or Cuba what it's like when the government can bend the laws to suit their own purposes.

"The law has to apply to everyone or it's not justice."

I had never really looked at it from that perspective before.

"Sorry, I didn't mean to ridicule you."

"Yeah, I get that a lot."

"So, do you see any loopholes in this case?"

"Unfortunately, no. It looks like everything was done by the book. Your Detective Blaylock dotted all his i's and crossed all his t's."

"I was afraid of that. He's a good cop.

"So is there any chance at all?"

"Yes there is, but it's not based on a procedural flaw. Our success or failure will depend on how the jury interprets the 'Castle Law'."

"What's that?"

"As you might surmise from the name, the whole concept is based on the idea that a man's home is his castle and he has the right to defend it from intruders.

"In 2007 the Missouri legislature passed its' version of the law, basically saying that a person can use physical force upon another person when and to the extent he *reasonably believes* such force to be necessary to defend himself or a third person from what he reasonably believes to be the use or imminent use of unlawful force by such other person."

"But that's what I did!" Mary protested.

"If you had shot him inside your home, we wouldn't be here today, but you didn't. The guy was running away and you chased him and shot him on the sidewalk.

"Our whole case will depend on our ability to convince a jury that your actions were reasonable and justifiable."

"Can we win?" I asked.

"It's a crap shoot. It all depends on the jury."

I looked at Mary. "I've seen this lady in the courtroom and she's a tiger. If anyone can get you off, it's her.

"Do you want to roll the dice or take the D.A.'s deal?"

"Hell no I ain't takin' no deal. Let's do it!"

I had to give Suzanne Romero credit. She had said our case depended not on the law but on winning the jury and by the day of the trial, the jury pool knew most everything there was to know about the lovable, seventy-three year old spinster that was being railroaded with a murder charge.

If the Mayor's agenda had been to get positive press from the case, just the opposite was occurring.

Letters to the editor and call-in talk shows gave unwavering support to the courageous old lady that had blown away an intruder.

We had hoped that with public opinion on our side, the Mayor would relent and drop the charges, but his position was that 'the law was the law' and he wasn't about to back down from his 'get tough against crime' policy.

The trial began the week before Christmas and we all kept our fingers crossed that Mary would be there to celebrate with us.

Bernard Larkin was a skilled attorney and wasted no time in establishing the groundwork for his case.

His first witness was Detective Blaylock.

"Detective, on the evening in question, when you arrived on the scene, what did you observe?"

"I saw a body laying in a pool of blood on the sidewalk in front of the Three Trails Hotel.

"The defendant, Mary Murphy, was sitting on the front step and a revolver was on the step beside her."

"What did you do then?"

"I approached Ms. Murphy and asked her what happened.

"She pointed to her front door and said that the victim ---"

"Objection!" Romero shouted. "The prosecution is characterizing Mario Bondell as a victim and clearly he was the aggressor and Ms. Murphy was the victim."

"Sustained. Please rephrase your question."

"So detective, what did Ms. Murphy tell you?"

"She said that Bondell had broken into her home, threatened her with a knife and took rent money which she had been collecting. She produced a pistol and Bondell fled."

"What did she say happened next?"

"She said that she pursued Bondell to her front porch and told him to stop. When he didn't stop, she fired her weapon striking Bondell. He fell to the sidewalk and died."

Shouts and cheers arose from the galley.

"ORDER!" barked the judge, banging his gavel. "If there is another such outburst, I will clear this courtroom! Proceed."

"Detective, how far was it from the porch to where Mr. Bondell was laying."

"Exactly twenty-three feet."

"So Mary Murphy admitted to shooting and taking the life of Mario Bondell?"

"Yes, she did."

He turned to Suzanne, "Your witness."

"Detective, you testified that Mario Bondell fled. When you were at the scene did the Medical Examiner determine where Bondell was shot?"

I could see Blaylock squirm in his chair. "He was shot in the chest."

"If he was fleeing, wouldn't the entry wound be in his back?"

"Uhhh, well there could be any number of reasons that the entry wound was in the chest."

"Really, name one!"

Larkin rose to his feet. "Objection. Calls for speculation."

"I'll say it does," she retorted. "I'll withdraw the question --- for now.

"When you examined the body, did you find a knife?"

"Yes, a switchblade knife was laying under Bondell's body."

"What else did you find?"

"There were several envelopes containing cash and there were names written on the outside.

"Detective, did you examine Ms. Murphy's front door?"

"Yes, it was apparent that there had been forced entry."

"And did you dust for prints?"

"Yes, we did find Mario Bondell's prints on the door."

"So, in your mind, is there any question that Mario Bondell forcibly entered Mary Murphy's apartment, threatened her and robbed her?"

"No, the evidence would support that."

"Thank you Detective. No further questions."

Larkin's next witnesses were the Medical Examiner and the CSI guy whose findings supported everything that had been said up to that point.

Then Larkin dropped the bomb.

"The prosecution calls Officer Walter Williams."

I looked at Suzanne and she shrugged her shoulders.

Larkin began by asking questions about how I knew Mary and our working relationship at the hotel.

Everything was pretty routine until finally, "Officer Williams, other than Mario Bondell, do you know of any other persons Mary Murphy has killed?"

Romero jumped to her feet.

"Objection, Your Honor! Ms. Murphy has no criminal record. This line of questioning is prejudicial."

Larkin was ready with a rebuttal. "Even though Ms. Murphy has never been convicted of a crime, Officer Williams' testimony will establish that three months ago she took the life of another man. Two persons dead at her hand are certainly enough to establish a pattern."

After a moment's thought, "I'll allow it."

"Mr. Williams, did you or did you not, witness Mary Murphy bludgeon a man to death with a baseball bat."

"Yes, but ---."

"That's all, Officer. Your witness."

I had seen Suzanne conferring with Mary and she approached me confidently.

"Mr. Williams, the prosecution would have us believe that Mary Murphy is a serial killer. Perhaps you can shed some light on the event Mr. Larkin described."

"I certainly can. The man was Uri Hassan. He was a hired assassin and had killed seven people in Kansas City including a doctor and a police officer.

"He was holding my wife and I at gunpoint and was about to pull the trigger when Mary hit him with the bat. My wife and I owe our lives to this woman's bravery."

I looked squarely at Larkin, "As I recall, Ms. Murphy received a letter of commendation from the City of Kansas City."

"Thank you, Officer. That's all."

Larkins next witness was Frederick Farnsworth.

I was shocked to see the tenant from room #7 take the stand.

"Mr. Farnsworth, you live at the Three Trails Hotel. Is that correct?"

"Yes, sir."

"And how do you know Mary Murphy?"

"She runs the place."

"And does she do a good job?"

"She sure does. She's a tough old cookie."

He gave Mary a wave and a smile.

"What do you mean by 'tough'?"

"Well, she don't take no crap off of no one that's for sure. And if one of us does somethin' bad, like pissing on the floor or throwing trash in the halls, she gets after us."

"Really? And how does she enforce that?"

"She's got this bat --- a really big one, and nobody wants to get on the bad side of Mary and her bat."

"So she threatens the tenants at the hotel with a bat?"

"Yep, and it works, too."

"Your witness."

"Mr. Farnsworth, do you like Mary Murphy?"

"Well sure! She's a sweet old gal."

"But you said she threatens you. Has she ever hit you with her bat?"

"No."

"Do you know of anyone she has ever hit with the bat?"

"Other than that killer guy, I can't say that I do."

"Do you think that she might?"

"Don't know for sure and don't want to find out."

"Thank you Mr. Farnsworth."

Larkin rested his case.

Suzanne Romero called her first witness, the officer who had taken the break-in call on Thanksgiving.

"Officer, were you dispatched to the Three Trails Hotel on Thanksgiving Day?"

"Yes."

"And what did you find?"

"Someone had forcibly entered Mary Murphy's apartment in her absence and had taken some money."

"Were any fingerprints found at the scene, and if so, could you identify them?"

"We found fingerprints, but they didn't match anyone in our system."

"Thank you, Officer."

Her next witness was the CSI at the shooting.

"Officer, you testified that you found Mario Bondell's fingerprints on the door casing the night he was shot. At my request, did you compare those prints with the prints found on the door on Thanksgiving Day?"

"We did."

"And what did you find?"

"Both prints were those of Mario Bondell."

"Thank you, Officer."

Romero's last witness was Mary herself.

Mary, how many times has someone broken into your home in the last four months?"

"Three times counting this last one."

"And what was different about the first two?"

"I wasn't home those times."

"Tell us in your own words what happened the night of the last break-in."

"I decided to go out and eat and take in a movie.

"I ate, but then I started gettin' the sniffles and sneezing, so I went back home.

"I made me a hot toddy, turned the lights down real low and was just sittin' there sipping my toddy and listening to Johnny Mathis when I heard something at the door.

"Johnny was just starting to sing *Misty* when this guy comes bustin' in the door.

"I don't know who was more surprised, him or me. I don't think he expected me to be home."

"What happened then?"

"When he sees me, he pulls out this knife --- you know --- one of them knives where you press a button and the blade pops out. Anyway, he points the knife at me and tells me that if I make a sound, he'll cut me, so I kept my mouth shut.

"Then he goes to the box under the slot in the door where the tenants put their rent and starts stuffin' the envelopes in his pockets.

"While he was doing that, I reached into my sewing basket and got my gun."

"Where did you get the gun?"

"From old man Feeney."

"Is he a gun dealer?"

"Heavens no! He's a tenant and lives upstairs. He give it to me after the second break-in. Said he didn't want nothin' to happen to me. It's a Colt .45

173

Peacemaker with ivory handles --- just like General Patton carried. He brung it home from the war."

"What did you do then?"

"I pointed the gun at the s.o.b. and told him to put Mr. Walt's money down and get his ass out of my apartment.

"But he didn't. He high-tailed it out of the door with all of Mr. Walt's rent money."

"What then?"

"I ran out on the porch and yelled at him to stop.

"He was on the sidewalk. He stopped all right. He turned around an flagged me a bird."

"Excuse me?"

"He gave me the finger --- like this." Mary said, extending the middle finger of her left hand.

"It means F---."

"That's okay, Mary. I think we know what it means. What happened then?"

"He held up that frog-sticker of his and said, "I'll be back, bitch."

"That's when I shot him."

"Were you afraid for your life?"

"Hell yes I was afraid. The man had been in my place three times, threatened to cut me and promised to come back and finish the job.

"Who wouldn't be scared?"

"Your witness."

Larkin started to get up, but then thought better of it. Mary was a sympathetic witness and badgering her would only make matters worse.

The judge recessed for lunch.

When the trial resumed, Larkin began his closing argument.

"There is no disputing the fact that Mary Murphy shot and killed Mario Bondell with a .45 caliber pistol.

"The commonwealth does not dispute the fact that Bondell had forcibly entered the residence and threatened Ms. Murphy.

"Defense council, in her closing argument, is going to use what's known as the 'Castle Law' to justify the murder.

"What you need to understand is that the Castle Law was created to protect citizens who were defending their homes, from being prosecuted.

"The law states that the person must be in 'imminent' danger and the protection under this law vanishes when the imminent threat is removed.

"In this case, Mario Bondell, seeing the gun, fled the scene. There was no longer an immediate threat.

"In fact, it was Mary Murphy who pursued Bondell who was nearly to the street, a full twenty-three feet from her porch, when he was shot.

"Had the shooting taken place inside the apartment, we wouldn't be here today, but the facts are that Mary Murphy pursued Bondell and took his life.

"Mary Murphy was no longer in danger and chose to take the law into her own hands.

"Mary Murphy is guilty of second degree murder."

Larkin took his seat and everyone's eyes went to Suzanne Romero.

"Mr. Larkin is correct. The Castle Law is most definitely our defense. It is there to protect citizens who are protecting their homes.

"It's always amusing when someone quotes a law and only quotes the part that supports his case.

"What Mr. Larkin failed to mention that Section 561.030 of our State Statute also says, 'a person may use physical force upon another person when she *reasonably believes* such force to be necessary to defend herself.

"That is the question before you today.

"Does the evidence support the notion that Mary Murphy could have reasonably believed that the action she took was necessary to defend herself?

"Put yourself in her shoes. The same man had broken into her home three times, and this last time threatened her with a switchblade knife.

"Furthermore, he promised to return.

"If you were Mary Murphy, would you believe that you were no longer in imminent danger?

"Or would you have reason to believe that as long as Mario Bondell was on the street, there was a clear and present danger?

"Mary Murphy is not a murderer. She is a sweet, seventy-three year old senior citizen who bravely fought off her attacker."

Then she looked directly at Larkin.

"The commonwealth, rather than bring murder charges against this woman, should be giving her another letter of commendation."

She was good! She was really good!

It took the jury less than an hour to bring a 'not guilty' verdict, and when it was read, the courtroom erupted in cheers.

On the way home, I marveled at how life can change your perspective on things.

A few months ago, I was cursing Suzanne Romero for helping dirt bags go free and today, she was my hero.

I thought about the blindfolded Lady Justice holding the scales, and I had a much deeper appreciation of what is involved in maintaining that delicate balance.

CHAPTER 13

Mary's arrest and trial had affected everyone in our little circle of friends.

Naturally, we were concerned about her and all of us were in court every day to give her moral support.

The trial ended five days before Christmas, but with everything going on, holiday preparations had taken a back seat.

Now that Mary was off the hook, we were free to turn our thoughts to more festive pursuits.

We decided to have a get together on Christmas Eve.

Everyone was invited including Ox's new squeeze and Ed, our new recruit.

Our little circle was growing larger.

The only no show was Vince who was going to Arizona to spend the holiday with his sister.

It was to be a simple affair. We would order pizza and Maggie and I would serve the drinks and everyone else would bring their favorite holiday goodies.

Jerry wanted to do the 'Secret Santa' thing, so we all put our names in the pot.

Maggie and I started assembling our assorted libations.

She mixed up a batch of holiday punch and I made sure there was plenty of Arbor Mist --- it goes great with pizza.

Of course there was the traditional eggnog and we had a bottle of Kahlua on hand in case someone felt that their nog needed an extra kick.

Ox and Judy had spent the day baking cookies. It was hard to imagine my robust friend rolling out dough, but I sensed that their domestic time together was a positive thing.

The Professor brought a fruitcake. I guess that was a throwback to his generation. I just hoped that somebody would eat a piece so that he wouldn't feel bad. I knew it wasn't going to be me.

Jerry brought a cake from the Price Chopper bakery that said 'Happy Birthday J'. He had rubbed out the rest of the name.

His justification was that Jason's family hadn't picked up the cake, so he got it for a really good price.

He then reminded us that Christmas was really a celebration of Jesus' birthday and that's what the 'J' stood for.

How could we argue with logic like that?

Willie brought a sweet potato pie.

He said that when he was a kid growing up, there were some years when all his family had were the vegetables that they had grown and stored, and his momma would bake that pie for their Christmas dessert.

I guess each of us have our own special memories of Christmases past.

Ed had stopped by the Cheesecake Factory and bought a Butterfinger cheesecake.

My mouth started watering the minute I saw it.

Dad announced that he and Bernice had spent the whole day making her fabulous 'female fudge'.

"What the heck is female fudge?" Jerry asked.

"No nuts!" Dad replied.

"So how do you know it's female fudge and not eunuch fudge?"

"Because we didn't make the fudge with nuts in the first place and then pick them out, smart ass. This fudge was born without nuts!"

The pizza guy showed up bearing boxes of the tasty pies and we all dug in.

As we were filling our plates, Jerry asked Willie if he knew what would happen if he ate the Christmas decorations.

Willie, of course, didn't have a clue.

"You'd get tinsel-itus!

"You're crazy, man! Get away from me!"

When we were all stuffed to the gills, Jerry announced that is was time to exchange gifts.

Apparently he had drawn my name and he looked on expectantly as I opened my gift.

It was a little box that had a guy on the front with the word 'Poof!' coming out his rear end.

I looked at him quizzically.

"It's a fart machine!" he announced. "Remote control --- you can put it under someone's chair and make it fart from across the room. Very high-tech --- much better than a whoopee cushion."

Maggie gave me the 'look'. "Don't even think about it!"

"Maybe you could use it at your squad room. I'll bet it would be a big hit."

"Yeah, I'm sure it would. Thanks, Jerry, I've always wanted one of these."

He beamed.

Dad had drawn Bernice's name and judging from the box, he had spent some time in Victoria's Secret.

Bernice squealed as she pulled the lacey thong from the box.

I had to look away. The last thing I wanted was the image of eighty-six year old Bernice wearing the thing burned into my memory.

Ox had drawn Judy's name and everyone 'awwwwed' when she pulled a charm bracelet from the box.

The charms were all miniature handguns, revolvers and automatics of every description.

"I love it!" she gushed and gave Ox a big kiss.

He blushed.

After all the gifts had been exchanged, Jerry strode to the center of the room with a small tablet in his hand.

"I wrote something special for our evening together. I hope you all enjoy it."

Twas the night before Christmas
And my friends are all here.
We'll laugh and have fun
And spread holiday cheer.

We're all overjoyed
To see our friend, Mary.
She just went through a trial
That was really quite scary.

There was a good lesson
That each of us learned.
Don't mess with this gal
Or you're gonna get burned.

There's Dad and Bernice
And I hope there's a chance
That before they arrive
He'll zip up his pants!

This year our friend Ox
Has got a new squeeze.
From what I've been told
The girl's quite a tease.

She'll laugh and she'll giggle
And call you sweet names
But if you get her pissed off
She'll blow out your brains!

And here's to Ed Jacobs
Our newest recruit.
He can kick a guy's ass
And he really can shoot.

As a brand new cop
He could sure raise the ante
If he could somehow arrest
That old vigilante.

And who could forget Willie
The guy from the street.
He's mended his ways
And he's really quite sweet.

Throughout our fine building
He's been known to roam.
All that we ask is
Keep your chitlins at home!

Then there's the Professor
Our venerable sage.
He gets around pretty good
For a man of his age.

With a good constitution
And a strong, healthy heart
He's in pretty good shape
For such an old fart!

Here's to Maggie and Walt
Our newly wed pair.
They've built their new nest
Up here in the air.

We all wish them well
In their life that's ahead.
And may they be happy
Especially in bed!

As I look around
At my friends that are here.
I know in my heart
They're the presents most dear.

And my Christmas prayer
And I know that it's right.
Is Merry Christmas to all
And to all a goodnight!

Everyone sat in silence.

The guy could be so goofy one minute and so lovable the next.

Spontaneously, we all started clapping and you could see the delight in Jerry's face.

Bernice looked at her watch. "It's time!"

"Time for what?" I asked.

"Santa Claus! He's started his trip from the North Pole!

"If we turn on the television, they show where he is right now!

"I used to watch that with my kids. Do you think we could turn it on?"

"Sure. Why not?"

I flipped on the TV, but instead of a big map following Santa's progress around the world, there was a breaking news bulletin.

A grim faced reporter was speaking.

"Hearts are heavy this evening as police arrested Father Angelo Brannigan, a priest at St. Sebastion Church in the Kansas City - St. Joseph Diocease.

"Two days ago, an alter boy at St. Sebastion reported being sexually abused by the cleric to his parents.

"Word spread quickly through the church and two more boys have come forward alleging similar abuse.

"The Bishop of the Diocese has not returned our calls."

I turned off the TV.

"How horrible!" Maggie said. "Especially on Christmas Eve."

"It's horrible anytime," Ox replied. "How many does this make? It seems like there's a new instance of abuse reported every week."

"It's not just the priests," Dad said. "A few weeks ago, a Boy Scout leader was arrested."

"Then there's the teachers," Judy said. "There's more and more of them having sex with their students."

Bernice was thoughtful, "When I was younger, I just don't remember all of this stuff going on. I wonder if this is something new or it just didn't get reported back then?"

185

Dad couldn't resist. "Well I sure don't remember teachers having sex with their students. If I had known that was going on, I might not have dropped out of school.

"Come to think of it, I can't remember any teacher that I would have wanted to have sex with."

"Dad, get serious!" I said.

"The pedophiles are the worst," Ox said. "Taking advantage of young kids --- probably scarring them for the rest of their lives."

The Professor joined the conversation. "To make matters worse, pedophiles are likely to be repeat offenders.

"Studies show that recidivism rates are estimated to be up to eighty-eight percent.

"If a guy does it once, he will most likely do it again."

The room suddenly became quiet.

Ed Jacobs had just been sitting there listening.

For the past year there had been numerous articles in the *Star* about priests who had committed sex crimes against children.

He remembered one specific article.

It stated that, *"---seven priests were accused after they died, four were in the process of being dismissed from the priesthood, six had retired and were later barred from the ministry, three of which had died, and two were on administrative leave."*

The thing that was missing from the article was any mention of them serving prison terms.

By the end of the conversation, he knew what he was going to do next.

CHAPTER 14

The Christmas season should be the most magical and joyous time of the year for children, but the news of the abuse by a trusted and revered member of the clergy cast a pall on the holiday celebrations.

In any society where children are entrusted to the care of religious leaders, teachers, coaches of sports teams and organizations such as the Boy Scouts, there has to be a level of confidence on the part of the parents that their children will be protected.

It is impossible for parents today to be with their children a hundred percent of the time, and when that trust is violated, the structure of our society is shaken to its' very foundation.

On Christmas Day, the Bishop of the Diocese, instead of celebrating the message of Jesus birth, held a news conference.

Without confirming or denying that the abuse had occurred, he said that the Diocese took the accusations very seriously and that they would be cooperating with the authorities to resolve the matter.

He also confirmed that Father Angelo Brannigan had been released on bail, but he had been relieved of his responsibilities and would remain in isolation at the St. Sebastion Convent during the investigation.

What he had not announced at the news conference was relayed to us at squad meeting by the captain.

"There is already public outrage over this scandal and if the accusations against Father Brannigan prove to be true, there will be overwhelming pressure to prosecute him to the fullest extent of the law.

"With the current climate of 'justice at any cost', the Bishop actually fears for Brannigan's life.

"Given the vigilante's penchant for executing the perpetrators of heinous crimes, it is not beyond the realm of possibility that he would go after Brannigan.

"That's why Brannigan is being sequestered at St. Sebastion's and the Diocese has asked the department, in return for their full co-operation, to provide round-the-clock protection.

"Given the high profile of this case, the last thing we need is for there to be another execution right under our noses, so the brass has instructed us to comply.

"The St. Sebastion complex is huge so there will be four officers on the scene at all times, two on the grounds and two within the complex.

"Unfortunately, that will require extra manpower so I'm afraid some of you will be doing some overtime. I'm sorry to take you away from your families during this holiday season, but sometimes that's the nature of the job.

"Your assignments are posted."

After the meeting, there was the usual grumbling that always occurs when schedules are disrupted.

It was actually my first day back to work following Mary's trial.

I wasn't sure how well I would be received given the fact that we had hired the nemesis of the department to defend Mary.

Most of the officers knew my old friend and had called to wish us well, but we had, in fact, employed the same tactics that rapists and druggies had used to set Mary free.

I got a lot of 'welcome backs' and 'congratulations' and my reputation didn't seem to be any worse for wear.

But the goodwill wasn't unanimous.

One grizzled old veteran that had been burned more than once by the lawyer's courtroom magic accosted me in the hall.

"Romero? Really? Do you know how many scumbags are walking the streets because of her?"

I looked him in the eye. "You know, I used to feel that way too, but this experience has helped me see things from a different point of view.

"We moan and groan when we see criminals exercising their right to a fair and competent defense, but let me tell you, you'll thank your lucky stars that we all have our constitutional rights when the shoe is on the other foot.

"I think the question is not 'how many scumbags are walking the streets because of her?' but rather, 'how many scumbags are walking the streets because we didn't do our job right?'"

As the old veteran walked away, I heard him mutter, "Damned liberal bleeding heart!"

Ox, who had been listening to the exchange observed, "Well, you can't please everyone."

While I was on leave for the trial, Ed, who had not yet been assigned a permanent partner, had been paired with Ox.

I was anxious to get his opinion of our new recruit.

"He'll make a good cop. He has good instincts and can handle himself remarkably well for an old guy."

"As opposed to me," I thought.

At the age of sixty-seven and weighing a buck forty-five dripping wet, I wasn't exactly an imposing figure.

"I'm glad to hear it. We C.R.A.P.pers have a reputation to uphold."

We looked at the schedule and saw that we had been assigned St. Sebastion duty that very day along with Ed and his new partner.

The St. Sebastion complex sat on twenty acres. It was composed of the church itself, a large gymnasium and a separate building that housed the convent.

It was an old complex and the grounds were covered with stately oaks surrounding a garden that was lovingly tended by the nuns.

If the vigilante was indeed interested in whacking Brannigan, there were plenty of places to hide.

His task would be more difficult if Brannigan would stay within the confines of the convent.

It would be next to impossible to penetrate our security and escape the notice of the nuns, even if, somehow, he managed to get inside.

It was cold outside, so the four of us decided to rotate our posts every two hours so that no one would freeze to death.

Ed and his partner took the first cold shift and Ox and I retreated into the bowels of the convent.

Ed Jacobs knew this job would be a challenge.

As he patrolled the perimeter of the complex, he could see that it would be no problem getting on the grounds.

Getting inside and finding Brannigan was another matter altogether.

The complex was so large that he and his partner had split up to cover more ground and he realized that he would be alone much of the time.

As he entered the garden, he marveled at its' beauty.

Even in the dead of winter, it was quite obvious that it had been tended with loving affection.

In one corner stood a small shed. On further inspection, he found that it held the shovels and rakes and other tools needed for the gardening.

A path led to the rear entrance of the convent. He made a mental note to find this door when it was his turn inside.

Precisely two hours from the beginning of the shift, the four officers met to exchange positions.

The interior of the convent was impressive.

Ed was not Catholic but he had traveled some, and his wife had always insisted that they visit the architectural wonders wherever they went.

She had dragged him through monasteries, cathedrals and museums all over the country.

This convent was not unlike many he had seen before.

On one end were the living quarters of the nuns and on the other was a chapel complete with stained glass and a confessional.

Presiding over all was the figure of Jesus on the cross.

At the rear of the building, a hallway led to store rooms, laundry and furnace room.

It was at the end of this hallway he found the door leading to the garden.

A plan began to take shape in his mind.

It was a bold plan that held more risk than anything he had attempted before, but if he were successful, this story of the vigilante would be remembered in police lore for years to come.

"As the old saying goes," he thought, *"No guts --- no glory!"*

Ed had been meticulous in his planning from the very beginning.

He had used disguises on several occasions when the chance of being seen was greater than usual and he had built quite an arsenal of weapons from untraceable sources such as estate sales and even Craig's list.

But the costume he needed now was not in his wardrobe and he had to shop.

If he was successful in this execution, the first thing the cops would do would be to canvass every costume shop in the city to try to find the guy who bought the frock of a priest.

He spent the morning transforming himself from Ed Jacobs to another persona that bore little resemblance to himself.

If surveillance cameras recorded him or chatty clerks remembered him, the description they would give would provide no clues as to his identity.

He found exactly what he was looking for in the fourth store he visited.

It was time to make his final preparations.

In a canvass bag, he placed the frock and the pieces of a disguise that could be quickly applied. The final item was a 9mm Glock with a silencer.

He was ready.

The next morning before squad meeting, Ed placed the canvass bag in the trunk of the cruiser that he and his partner would be using that day.

When the four officers arrived at St. Sebastian's, he and his partner took the first outside shift.

As before, they split up and when he knew that he was alone, he removed the canvass bag from the trunk and hid it in the corner of the shed behind some bags of mulch.

In two hours, they exchanged places and as soon as Ed was alone, he made his way to the back door and retrieved the canvass bag.

In a back corner of the furnace room, he donned the frock of a priest and applied a mustache and goatee.

He slipped the Glock into his belt underneath the frock and headed toward the dormitory.

His partner was standing by the entrance of the convent and barely gave him a glance as he walked by.

He met a nun coming down the hall.

"Sister, I am Father Aequitas from Chicago. I have been asked to speak with Father Brannigan. Can you direct me to his room?"

She complied without question and in a moment Ed was standing outside Brannigan's door.

He knocked and Brannigan had a puzzled look on his face seeing the strange cleric.

"I'm Father Aequitas from the Chicago Diocese. The Bishop asked me to come.

"I have had some experience in --- uhh --- matters of this kind and he thought I might be of some help. May I come in?"

Brannigan stood aside and Ed entered the room.

"I --- I don't understand. Why exactly are you here?"

"I'm sure that you are aware of the delicate nature of this situation.

"Not only are you personally in deep trouble, but this whole incident casts a bad light on the Kansas City Diocese and the Church as a whole."

"Yes, I'm aware of all that."

"My task here is to give the Bishop some direction in how to proceed and how best to mitigate the damage to the Church, but I am also here for you.

"Regardless of how this plays out, you will need the help and support of the Church. Whether you are guilty or innocent, the Bishop is concerned for your mortal soul. You are still a child of God."

"So what am I to do?"

"You know as well as I that the best way to ease a troubled soul is to cast your burden on the Lord --- seek his guidance and ask for his mercy on your soul.

"In your ministry, you have told many a parishioner to confess his sins and seek penance from the Lord, and now it is time to take your own advice."

"You've come to hear my confession?"

"The Bishop thought it might be easier to share your burden with a stranger."

"I --- I don't know."

"You know that absolution only comes with confession and a genuine remorse for your sins. It is one thing to be judged guilty by men and quite another to be found wanting in the eyes of God."

"Yes, you are right, of course."

"Good! Then let us proceed."

They made their way to the confessional and each took their place.

Ed slid the window opened. "I'm ready, my son."

"Bless me Father, for I have sinned. It has been three years since my last confession."

"Go on."

There was a long silence.

"I don't want to do it. I know that it's wrong, but I just can't help myself."

"What is it that is wrong."

"The boys --- I see them and something just comes over me."

"So the boys who have come forth are telling the truth?"

"Yes --- I tried to stop but it just keeps happening."

"So have there been others?"

"Yes, since the early days of my priesthood. Is there any penance that can atone for what I have done? Is there any chance for absolution?"

Ed had the confession that he had needed. He knew that sometimes people are wrongly accused and the last thing he wanted to do was execute an innocent priest.

He cracked open the door of the confessional and seeing no one, he replied, "Yes, there is indeed a penance that is appropriate for your sins and with this penance you will sin no more."

He drew the 9mm from under his frock and fired two rounds through the wall of the confessional.

He heard Brannigan slump against the wall.

"May God have mercy on your soul."

Quietly he retreated to the furnace room, stuffed the frock, gun and disguise in the bag and stowed it in the tool shed.

A moment later, he met his partner in the foyer. It was time to trade places again.

It would not be until late in the evening shift that someone would discover that the vigilante had struck again.

Chapter 15

Once again, Maggie and I had just settled in for a quiet evening alone when the phone rang.

It was the captain.

Father Brannigan had been found shot to death in the confessional at St. Sebastion's Convent.

The vigilante had struck again.

According to the Medical Examiner, the time of death was during my shift, and the four of us were being ordered back to the scene for questioning.

Great! It seemed that I just couldn't catch a break.

I quickly dressed and headed to the convent.

I was the last to arrive and joined the group consisting of the captain, the Bishop, Ox, Ed and his partner.

The M.E. had just loaded the body onto a gurney.

We watched as the body was wheeled to the waiting meat wagon.

The captain turned to us. "How could this have happened?"

None of us uttered a word.

Just then, a nun hurried up to the Bishop.

"This is just horrible! Is Father Aequitas all right?"

The Bishop looked puzzled. "Who is Father Aequitas?"

Now it was the nun's turn to look puzzled. "He was here this afternoon. He said that he was from the Chicago Diocese and that you had sent for him to talk to Father Brannigan. I directed him to his room."

A strange look came over the Bishop's face. "Aequitas --- that's the Latin word for 'justice'."

The captain shook his head, "So the vigilante was dressed as a priest? How could we have overlooked that possibility?"

He turned to us. "Did any of you see a priest this afternoon?"

Ed's partner raised his hand. "I saw a priest this afternoon, but I didn't think anything of it. There have been priests and nuns all over the place every day we've been here.

"He was alone, but then later I saw him with Father Brannigan. They walked by the foyer on the way to the chapel."

"What did he look like?"

"Well, he was wearing one of those robe things that priests wear --- he was a white guy --- older --- and he had a mustache and goatee. That's about all I can remember."

He turned to the nun, "Is that the man you talked to?"

"Yes, that's him exactly."

"Can you remember anything else?"

"Well, he seemed really nice."

The captain just shook his head.

Each of us was questioned but Ed's partner was the only one who saw the guy.

As soon as the media got hold of the story, the proverbial poop hit the fan.

Once again, the department was held up to ridicule for not being able to protect a priest locked away in a convent.

Even worse, the vigilante was being heralded as a hero for administering justice for the abused children.

It was a city divided.

The only good thing to come out of Brannigan's murder was the return to our regular shifts.

With New Year's just a few days away, we were all glad that there was no more overtime.

I looked forward to relaxing and celebrating the holiday with Maggie.

Weeks ago I had made reservations at Ruth's Chris Steakhouse on the Country Club Plaza.

It was one of our favorite places to eat, but we never got out the door for less than a hundred and fifty bucks, so we saved it for special occasions.

On the day before New Year's Eve, as soon as I saw Ox, I knew something was wrong.

"Hey, Buddy, why the long face?"

"New Year's Eve. I totally screwed it up."

"How so? Aren't you and Judy going out?"

"We have a date, but with all the stuff going on, I totally forgot to make reservations and now I can't get us in anywhere. Everything's full."

The look on the big guy's face broke my heart.

"Look, Maggie and I are going to Ruth's Chris on the Plaza. I'll call and see if I can get a table for four instead of a table for two."

"You'd do that?"

"Sure, no problem."

Easier said than done.

They too were booked up and it was a table for two or nothing.

I called Maggie and explained the situation. I was surprised at her response.

"Cancel the Plaza. We'll do something else."

"What?"

"What's more important, one meal at a fancy restaurant or supporting your partner? We can go to Ruth's Chris another time."

"Yeah, I guess you're right."

My mind was on the three inch filet mignon sizzling on the hot plate of melted butter that I was not going to be eating, when I got back to Ox.

"No tables available, but if it's okay with you, Maggie and I would like to join you and Judy. We'll find someplace to go."

"No, that's just not right."

"But it's what we want to do."

"Thank you."

I could see the look of relief on his face.

It turned out that the best we could do was my favorite haunt, Mel's Diner on Broadway.

The food was always delicious, but the ambiance was a world apart from the famous steakhouse.

Ox picked up Judy and met us at Mel's.

It was Judy's first visit to the diner and she seemed eager to delve into the wonderful world of comfort food.

Everything at Mel's is either deep fried or cooked in butter on a big grill. It may not be the healthiest food in the world, but you always leave very full and very satisfied.

At my urging, Judy had ordered the chicken fried steak with mashed potatoes smothered in cream gravy.

Her 'ooohs' and 'aaahs' as she tasted each bite led me to believe that she was not disappointed.

We had just polished off our main course and were busy trying to decide which of Mel's home made pies we wanted to order, when a figure walked into the diner.

Every eye in the place was on him immediately.

He just didn't fit.

While everyone else in the diner was dressed in jeans and casual clothes, this guy looked like he had just stepped out of a Calvin Klein ad.

He was tall with rugged good looks and a body that could only have come from hours in the gym.

He was a stud and he definitely knew it.

His gaze drifted from one patron to the next until his eyes locked on Judy.

"Oh crap!" she said, slumping in her seat.

The guy wasted no time approaching our table.

"Judy!" he said, smiling through perfect white teeth.

"Derek! What are you doing here?"

"I was hoping you had come to your senses."

He looked disparagingly around the diner and then his eyes focused on Ox.

"So is this the best you could come up with?"

She ignored the insult. "Have you been following me?"

"Let's just say that I've been keeping tabs on you and when I saw you in this pitiful place on New Year's Eve --- well, I couldn't help but come to your rescue.

"My current employer has rented the penthouse at the President Hotel and is hosting a party there and ---."

"You pompous bastard! How dare you barge in here and disturb our dinner!"

He reached for her arm, "Let me take you away from all this."

She jerked away, "Don't you touch me."

Ox calmly put his hand on her arm, "Let me handle this."

The big man stood and looked Derek in the eye, "I don't know who you are and I don't much care, but it's quite apparent that you're upsetting my date and I think you should leave."

Derek looked down at Judy, "So now you're letting Neanderthals speak for you?"

That was the last straw for Ox.

Using his most intimidating big boy voice cultivated from twenty-four years of patrolling the streets, "That's it, Pal!

"You've definitely worn out your welcome. If you're not out of here in the next five seconds, you're going to be wearing a corsage of Mel's chicken gravy on that fancy suit and that pretty smile will be missing some teeth. Do I make myself clear?"

Apparently, he had made his intent crystal clear and Derek wanted no part of it.

"Very well then, I'll leave." Then turning to Judy, "You'll regret this someday."

He turned and stalked out of the diner.

The patrons at the other booths applauded and Mel showed up at our table with huge slabs of pie.

"On the house." he said.

Judy was visibly shaken and Maggie took her hand, "Who was that guy?"

"Ex-boyfriend --- a big mistake. I was doing some off-duty security work at the auto show. Derek was a model and spokesperson for BMW. We got to talking and well --- you can see how a girl could be impressed. The guy drives a Ferrari, for gosh sakes.

"We went out a few times, fancy places with all the trimmings, but I came to realize that I was just another 'thing' to him, like his fancy car and his jewelry.

"I tried to break it off, but as you could see, he's not used to taking 'no' for an answer. That's why I moved here from north of the river. I wanted to get away from him."

"Maybe Ox got the message across," I said.

Judy took his hand, "Thank you. You were wonderful."

Ox looked depressed. "How can I ever compete with a Ferrari and a penthouse at the President? I'm just a lousy beat cop."

Judy smiled, "You big goof! You just don't get it, do you? Hang on for a minute."

She slid out of the seat and went to the big jukebox in the back of the diner.

After flipping through the selections, she deposited her coins and pushed the buttons.

Soon, the beautiful voice of Patsy Cline filled the diner.

The song was about a woman who must choose between love and riches.

The song ended with the soulful words,

"And the hand that brings the rose tonight, is the hand I will hold.

For the rose of love means more to me, than any rich man's gold."

"Now do you get it?"

A tear rolled down the big man's cheek.

We all went back to our apartment after dinner.

We popped open a bottle of Arbor Mist and chatted while we awaited the magical hour.

The end of the year is always a time for reflection on the events of the past and our hopes of events to come.

It was hard to believe that we had crammed so much into one year.

"The best thing that happened to me this year was getting hitched to this wonderful woman," I said, taking Maggie's hand.

"Even though it meant getting abducted by Hawaiian zealots and escaping from a dormant volcano," Maggie replied, shaking her head.

Judy's mouth dropped open. "You've gotta tell me that story."

It took a half hour to share the adventures of our Hawaiian wedding.

"Don't forget about blowing up the lake in Loose Park," Ox said laughing.

"That was you guys! I want details."

It took another half hour to tell her about the religious nuts who tried to blow up Kansas City.

By the time we had finished reminiscing about the 'sting' that had brought a huge pharmaceutical company to its knees, it was almost midnight.

We refilled our glasses and toasted the New Year as the clock struck twelve.

We hugged and kissed and declared that the evening had been a great success.

After my friends left, I thought about all the drama that had filled our lives this past year and I secretly hoped that the year to come would be a bit less traumatic.

But it wasn't to be.

CHAPTER 16

The New Year was off to a lousy start.

A cold front and winter storm had moved into the region late on New Year's Day and by the time Ox and I were on patrol, freezing drizzle was turning into snow.

Traffic was at a crawl and the radio had been busy directing the traffic guys to fender benders all over the city.

We had just pulled into Dunkin Donuts for a cup of joe and a long john when the radio crackled again.

"Shots fired at the bodega on Southwest Boulevard. All units in the area respond."

We were just a few blocks away.

"Car 54 responding."

We parked in front of the bodega and everything looked quiet inside.

We drew our weapons and moved cautiously to each side of the door.

Ox leaned in for a look and whispered, "Body."

Seeing no movement inside, we entered and made a sweep of the retail area.

We found a second body on the floor behind the checkout counter.

"Call it in," I whispered. "I'll check the back."

I moved through the door into the storeroom. There were rows of shelves holding boxes of cereal, candy bars and chips.

At the far end was the door to a bathroom that stood partially open and the exit door to the alley that ran behind the store.

I made my way to the bathroom and was about to peek inside when I heard a rustle behind me.

Out of the corner of my eye I saw a figure charging toward me with a crowbar poised in mid air.

I ducked and took a glancing blow to my shoulder.

It hurt like hell, but the momentum carried my attacker past me and I jumped on his back.

Only it wasn't a he --- it was a young woman.

I wrestled the crowbar from her hand and she began to swing wildly with her fists.

By this time, Ox was on the scene and helped me restrain the woman.

"Calm down!" he ordered. "We're the police!"

The woman looked dazed. "You're cops? You're not Cruz's men?"

"You're okay," I reassured her. "Everything's going to be okay."

"Mario!" She became agitated again. "Where's Mario?"

I looked at Ox. Neither of us wanted to break the bad news.

By this time, the place was crawling with cops and Detective Blaylock appeared on the scene.

Medics checked the woman whose name was Rosa Alverez.

After determining that she had not sustained any injuries, Blaylock began his interrogation.

"Ms. Alverez, can you tell us what happened here?"

"I came by the store to see Mario --- we are --- were engaged." She began to weep.

"We're truly sorry for your loss. What happened next?"

"Mario was stocking the candy rack. His father, Manuel, said that we could talk after the stocking was done. Mario asked me to go to the storeroom and bring a box of Milky Way bars.

"I was searching for the bars when I heard someone enter the store.

"I peeked around the corner and saw that it was Hector Cruz. I was afraid so I stayed in the back."

"Why were you afraid?"

"Hector Cruz is a very bad man. Everyone fears him."

"Go on."

"I heard Hector ask Manuel for his payment, but Manuel told him that he was paying no more.

"They argued and I saw Hector pull a gun from his pants and shoot Manuel.

"I ran to the back of the storeroom and hid behind a big tissue box. Then I heard the second shot and feared for Mario's life.

"I heard footsteps coming into the storeroom but I was very quiet and he did not see me.

"Then the police came." She looked at me, "So sorry, I thought ---."

"It's okay," I said, rubbing my shoulder. "You did the right thing."

"So you can positively identify Hector Cruz as the man who shot Manuel Gonzales?"

"Yes, it was him!"

At that moment, Antonio Vargas, the head guy in the gang task force, came through the door.

"Whatcha got?"

"Hey, Tony. I think we've got a hot one for you."

After Blaylock had shared what we had discovered, Vargas rubbed his hands together.

"Maybe we've got that bastard at last.

"Cruz is the undisputed leader of the Latino gangs on the West side. He's mean --- nobody wants to mess with him.

"He's involved in everything that's dirty on this side of town.

"He's been arrested three times and we thought we had him cold each time, but our eye witnesses either recanted their stories or wound up dead.

"He skated every time."

I looked at poor Rosa Alverez sitting in a daze across the room.

She was probably thinking that her ordeal was over, but it was just beginning.

Knowing full well the outcome of Cruz's previous trials, Rosa Alverez was placed into protective custody.

She was sequestered in a safe house with two armed officers on duty around the clock.

Given the fact that our last protective detail was a total failure, every one of us assigned to the safe house took nothing for granted.

All went according to plan and there were no incidents leading up to the trial.

Ox and I being the first officers on the scene were seated in the courtroom along with Rosa and Manuel Gonzales' widow.

The prosecution called the usual witnesses, the Medical Examiner to establish time and cause of death, and the CSI guy to testify about the evidence at the crime scene.

After each of them had testified, defense council asked the same question in his cross-examination, "Did you find anything in your investigation that would directly connect my client, Mr. Cruz, to these brutal murders?"

The answer in both cases was 'no'.

Then I heard the Prosecuting Attorney call my name.

After I was sworn in, he asked me to relate what I had witnessed on the day of the murders.

I told my story from the time we received the call to the moment when Rosa Alverez attacked me with the crowbar.

"When Rosa realized that you were policemen, what did she tell you?"

Defense council jumped to his feet. "Objection! Hearsay!"

"Sustained!"

"Officer Williams, did Rosa Cruz tell you she had witnessed Hector Alvarez shoot Manuel Gonzales?"

"OBJECTION! Your honor?"

"Mr. Prosecutor, I will not warn you again." Then to the jury, "You will disregard this last question."

Seeing that he had taken me as far as I could go, he turned me over to the defense.

"Officer Williams, when you arrived at the scene, did you see my client Hector Cruz?"

"No."

"Did you find any evidence linking my client to these murders?"

"Only the testimony of an eyewitness."

"No further questions."

The judge turned to the Prosecuter, "Any more witnesses?"

"Yes, your honor, one more. The prosecution calls Rosa Alverez to the stand."

The judge looked at his watch and realizing that this final witness was going to take a lot of time, declared, "One moment counselor. Due to the lateness of the hour, we will resume testimony tomorrow morning."

He banged his gavel. "Court dismissed!"

As Hector Cruz was being led out of the courtroom, he paused in front of Rosa Alverez, raised his arm toward her and pointed his fingers like a gun. He drew back his thumb and as it snapped forward, you could see him mouth the word, 'Bang!'

Poor Rosa was visibly shaken and I didn't blame her.

It was going to be another long day.

Ox and I had been in the courtroom all day and we had drawn guard duty at the safe house for the night shift.

More overtime.

I had six hours to get home, grab a bite to eat and get a few hours sleep before reporting to the safe house at midnight.

As I drove to the safe house, I reviewed the day's trial.

It was quite obvious that the prosecution's entire case rested on Rosa's testimony.

Once she was on the stand, a 'guilty' verdict was a slam-dunk, but it was nine long hours until that would happen and a lot could transpire in nine hours.

Three other trials had come down to this and three times Cruz had walked away.

Rosa Alverez had to be protected and Ox and I had to do it.

Ed Jacobs had followed the case from the beginning.

When he had seen the photos of the bodies of Manuel and Mario Gonzales and met Rosa Alverez, he wanted more than anything to see that Hector Cruz got what was coming to him.

He had wracked his brain trying to find a way to get to Cruz, but security was tighter than ever before.

After the Brannigan fiasco, the department wasn't about to lose another prisoner.

He had taken his turn at guarding the safe house and although there had been no problems, the place was far from impenetrable.

Ed had been sitting in the back of the courtroom during the day's trial and he had seen Cruz point his finger-gun at Rosa.

Ed had seen no fear in Cruz's eyes and it was if he knew that the woman would not be there to testify against him the next day.

If he could not get to Cruz, the next best thing was to make sure that Rosa was alive to put the bastard in jail.

He gathered his gear and headed to the safe house.

He dressed as warm as he could, knowing that he would spend the night patrolling the perimeter of the house.

After dark, it was easy to conceal himself in the shadows.

The evening had been quiet and just before midnight, he saw Ox and Walt arrive to begin their shift.

He watched as the taillights of the cruiser from the earlier shift disappeared into the night.

He fought to stay awake and alert, but the cold and long hours were taking their toll.

Then, just before sunrise, he saw headlights coming toward the house.

He looked at his watch. It was time for the shift change.

Just a few more hours and they would be home free.

But where was Cruz? Why hadn't he made a move?

The headlights suddenly stopped. Why would they stop?

Quietly, he made his way toward the cruiser, but just before he reached it, the cruiser came around the corner.

He ducked behind a tree and watched as the car drove by.

Something was wrong! He didn't know the officers in the cruiser. The captain had been rotating the same men, trying to keep Rosa comfortable with familiar faces.

He raced to where he had seen the cruiser stop and quickly searched the ditch along the side of the road.

There, to his horror, he found the bodies of the two officers who were to take the next shift.

Cruz was making his move.

He hoped that he wasn't too late.

Drawing his gun, he raced toward the safe house.

As he turned the corner, he saw Walt open the door and invite the imposters inside.

"Just a couple of hours to go," I said as Rosa emerged from her room.

Ox and I had not slept at all and Rosa had slept fitfully.

"Why don't you grab some breakfast?" Ox asked. "The next shift will be here soon and they'll be taking you to the courthouse."

Just then we saw the reflection of headlights turning into the driveway.

Ox peeked out of the window. "It's the cruiser."

I was tired and hungry, but mostly I was relieved when Ox made that announcement. The pressure had been almost unbearable. The last thing we wanted was for Rosa to be hurt on our watch.

We heard the car doors shut and a minute later there was a tap on the door.

I took a quick look through the peephole in the door and saw two uniformed officers. They had turned and were looking down the driveway. I only saw their backs.

I slipped off the chain lock, flipped the deadbolt and opened the door.

"Come on --- ."

Before the words were out of my mouth, two guys that I had never seen before burst into the room with guns drawn.

One of the men had his gun trained on me and the other was pointing at Ox.

"Let's get those guns on the floor nice and slow," the bigger one said.

I looked at Ox, but we both knew that they had us cold.

We pulled our guns with two fingers and tossed them on the floor.

"Now kick them over here."

We complied.

"Hands behind your head."

When our fingers were locked behind our heads, he motioned to the other guy.

"Get the girl."

The man looked in the bedroom and not finding her there moved to the kitchen.

We heard a 'thunk' and the sounds of a struggle. It sounded like Rosa was putting up a fight.

Then we heard a slap and a sharp scream and a moment later the man drug Rosa out by the arm.

He had stuck his gun in his pants and was holding her with one hand and a knot on his head with the other.

"The little bitch whacked me with a pan."

"Then you can have the first turn at her after we eliminate these two."

The big guy pointed his gun at me and pulled back the hammer.

"Adios, cop."

I braced myself for the inevitable, but before he could pull the trigger, the door burst open and a figure came flying across the room.

The gunman turned toward the intruder and took the full impact of the charge.

They both went down and as they hit the floor, I heard the report as the gun discharged and I saw the body of the intruder convulse as the slug from the big Glock ripped through his body.

Ox wasted no time getting to the guy holding Rosa whose gun was still tucked into the waistband of his pants and I pounced on the guy on the floor who was desperately trying to roll the limp body off his chest.

After both men were cuffed, I finished rolling the body of the man who had saved our lives onto his back.

I found myself staring into the glazed eyes of Ed Jacobs.

He was still breathing --- barely.

I gathered him into my arms and his eyelids fluttered.

"Ed! What are you doing here?"

I had to lean close to hear his rasping words.

"Cruz --- I knew he would be coming --- figured you might need some backup."

"Ed, you saved all of us. Hang in there, Buddy!"

I felt his body quiver.

"We're --- we're gonna get --- the bastard --- aren't ----------- we?"

A long sigh escaped his lips and his body went limp.

"Yeah, Ed, we're going to get him."

I wept as my newest recruit lay dead in my arms.

EPILOGUE

A stunned Hector Cruz sat in shock when Rosa Alverez walked into the courtroom.

Her testimony led to the conviction of a criminal who had eluded punishment for years.

Cruz is currently housed on death row in the Potosi Correctional Center awaiting execution.

All this was made possible by the heroic actions of Ed Jacobs.

Ed, along with the other two officers slain that day, were given a funeral honoring the fallen heroes.

Ed was awarded the Medal of Honor posthumously.

As I stood in the cold, listening to the strains of the bagpipes as they played *Amazing Grace*, my thoughts were on how our lives hang in the balance every day.

If Ed had been just ten seconds later, it would have been me in that flag draped casket and my new bride would be grieving at my graveside.

As I looked back over the events of the past few months, I couldn't help but play the 'what if' game.

What if we had never volunteered to help at the Salvation Army soup kitchen?

We would never have met Ed.

What if that punk had not tried to cut Mary and Ed had not come to her rescue?

Ed would never have been asked to be a cop.

What if Ed had never become a cop?

I looked again at the casket poised over the gaping hole in the ground --- that would be me.

As the bugler's last notes of *Taps* faded away, I couldn't help but wonder what forces were at work that help Lady Justice keep those delicate scales in balance.

Mysteriously, the vigilante killings ceased as abruptly as they had begun.

Some speculated that he had moved on to another city, while others believed that he had made his point and was quietly watching until he was needed again, but no one knew for sure.

There were indeed positive results from his presence in our city.

After Bernhard Goetz rallied the citizens of New York as the 'Subway Vigilante', the crime rate diminished significantly.

The same phenomena occurred in Kansas City. Incidents of violent crime dropped to almost half of what they had been before his arrival.

His proponents were quick to point out that the only persons who died at his hand were hardened criminals, some of whom had slipped through the fingers of the law.

His champions said that while our justice system was plodding and often ineffectual, his was swift and sure.

Plato wrote in *The Republic*, that the best form of government is a benevolent dictatorship.

While it may certainly be the most efficient in a perfect world, ours is certainly not a perfect world and history reminds us that men who hold the power of life and death in their hands rarely, if ever, use that power for the greater good.

It is certainly a frightening notion to think that any single individual could arbitrarily assume the mantle of judge, jury and executioner and wield that power with impunity.

Suzanne Romero, who was often cursed and vilified for defending the criminal element, taught me a valuable lesson.

Unless our constitutional rights and basic freedoms are guaranteed for *every* man, it could be just a matter of time before they are not available to *any* man.

Protecting those rights and our system of justice is the responsibility of every citizen, but there are some who take that responsibility a step further.

My name is Walt Williams and that's why I'm a cop.

ABOUT THE AUTHOR

Award-winning author, Robert Thornhill, began writing at the age of sixty-six, and in four short years has penned thirteen novels in the Lady Justice mystery/comedy series, the seven volume Rainbow Road series of chapter books for children, a cookbook and a mini-autobiography.

The fifth, sixth, seventh, ninth and tenth novels in his Lady Justice series, *Lady Justice and the Sting, Lady Justice and Dr. Death, Lady Justice and the Vigilante, Lady Justice and the Candidate* and *Lady Justice and the Book Club Murders* won the Pinnacle Achievement Award from the National Association of Book Entrepreneurs as the best mystery novels in 2011, 2012 and 2013.

Robert holds a master's degree in psychology, but his wit and insight come from his varied occupations including thirty years as a real estate broker.

He lives with his wife, Peg, in Independence, Mo.

LADY JUSTICE TAKES A. C.R.A.P.
City Retiree Action Patrol

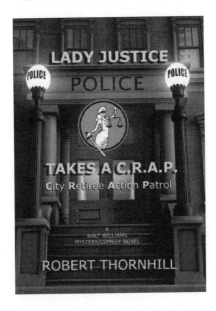

This is where it all began.

See how sixty-five year old Walt Williams became a cop and started the City Retiree Action Patrol.

Meet Maggie, Willie, Mary and the Professor, Walt's sidekicks in all of the Lady Justice novels.

Laugh out loud as Walt and his band of Senior Scrappers capture the Realtor Rapist and take down the Russian Mob.

http://booksbybob.com/lady-justice-takes-a-crap-3rd_383.html

LADY JUSTICE AND THE LOST TAPES

In Lady Justice and the Lost Tapes, Walt and his band of scrappy seniors continue their battle against the forces of evil.

When an entire Eastside Kansas City neighborhood is terrorized by the mob, Walt must go undercover to solve the case.

Later, the amazing discovery of a previously unknown recording session by a deceased rock 'n' roll idol stuns the music industry.

http://booksbybob.com/lady-justice-and-the-lost-tapes_307.html

LADY JUSTICE GETS LEI'D

In *Lady Justice Gets Lei'd*, Walt and Maggie plan a romantic honeymoon on the beautiful Hawaiian islands, but ancient artifacts discovered in a cave in a dormant volcano and a surprising revelation about Maggie's past, lead our lovers into the hands of Hawaiian zealots.

http://booksbybob.com/lady-justice-gets-leid_309.html

LADY JUSTICE AND THE AVENGING ANGELS

Lady Justice has unwittingly entered a religious war.

Who better to fight for her than Walt Williams?

The Avenging Angels believe that it's their job to rain fire and brimstone on Kansas City, their Sodom and Gomorrah.

In this compelling addition to the Lady Justice series, Robert Thornhill brings back all the characters readers have come to love for more hilarity and higher stakes.

You'll laugh and be on the edge of your seat until the big finish.

Don't miss *Lady Justice and the Avenging Angels!*

http://booksbybob.com/lady-justice-and-the-avenging-angels_336.html

LADY JUSTICE AND THE STING

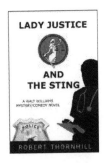

BEST NEW MYSTERY NOVEL ---WINTER 2012

National Association of Book Entrepreneurs

In *Lady Justice and the Sting*, a holistic physician is murdered and Walt becomes entangled in the high-powered world of pharmaceutical giants and corrupt politicians.

Maggie, Ox Willie, Mary and all your favorite characters are back to help Walt bring the criminals to justice in the most unorthodox ways.

A dead-serious mystery with hilarious twists!

http://booksbybob.com/lady-justice-and-the-sting_348.html

LADY JUSTICE AND DR. DEATH

Best New Mystery Novel – Fall 2011

North American Bookseller's Exchange

In *Lady Justice and Dr. Death*, a series of terminally ill patients are found dead under circumstances that point to a new Dr. Death practicing euthanasia in the Kansas City area.

Walt and his entourage of scrappy seniors are dragged into the 'right-to-die' with dignity controversy.

The mystery provides a light-hearted look at this explosive topic and death in general.

You may see end-of-life issues in a whole new light after reading *Lady Justice and Dr. Death*.
http://booksbybob.com/lady-justice-and-dr-death_351.html

LADY JUSTICE AND THE WATCHERS

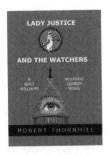

Suzanne Collins wrote *The Hunger Games*, Aldous Huxley wrote *Brave New World* and George Orwell wrote *1984*.

All three novels were about dystopian societies of the future.

In *Lady Justice and the Watchers*, Walt sees the world we live in today through the eyes of a group who call themselves 'The Watchers'.

Oscar Levant said that there's a fine line between genius and insanity.

After reading *Lady Justice and the Watchers*, you may realize as Walt did that there's also a fine line separating the life of freedom that we enjoy today and the totalitarian society envisioned in these classic novels.

Quietly and without fanfare, powerful interests have instituted policies that have eroded our privacy, health and individual freedoms.

Is the dystopian society still a thing of the distant future or is it with us now disguised as a wolf in sheep's clothing?

http://booksbybob.com/lady-justice-and-the-watchers_365.html

LADY JUSTICE AND THE CANDIDATE

BEST NEW MYSTERY NOVEL – FALL 2012

National Association of Book Entrepreneurs

Will American politics always be dominated by the two major political parties or are voters longing for an Independent candidate to challenge the establishment?

Everyone thought that the slate of candidates for the presidential election had been set until Benjamin Franklin Foster came on the scene capturing the hearts of American voters with his message of change and reform.

Powerful interests intent on preserving the status quo with their bought-and-paid-for politicians were determined to take Ben Foster out of the race.

The Secret Service comes up with a quirky plan to protect the Candidate and strike a blow for Lady Justice.

Join Walt on the campaign trail for an adventure full of surprises, mystery, intrigue and laughs!

http://booksbybob.com/lady-justice-and-the-candidate_367.html

LADY JUSTICE AND THE
BOOK CLUB MURDERS

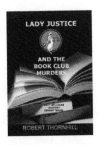

Best New Mystery Novel – Spring 2013

Members of the Midtown Book Club are found murdered.

It is just the beginning of a series of deaths that lead Walt and Ox into the twisted world of a serial killer.

In the late 1960's, the Zodiac Killer claimed to have killed 37 people and was never caught --- the perfect crime.

Oscar Roach, dreamed of being the next serial killer to commit the perfect crime.

He left a calling card with each of his victims --- a mystery novel, resting in their blood-soaked hands.

The media dubbed him 'The Librarian'.

Walt and the Kansas City Police are baffled by the cunning of this vicious killer and fear that he has indeed committed the perfect crime.

Or did he?

Walt and his wacky senior cohorts prove, once again, that life goes on in spite of the carnage around them.

The perfect blend of murder, mayhem and merriment.

http://booksbybob.com/lady-justice-and-the-book-club-murders_370.html

LADY JUSTICE AND THE CRUISE SHIP MURDERS

Ox and Judy are off to Alaska on a honeymoon cruise and invite Walt and Maggie to tag along.

Their peaceful plans are soon shipwrecked by the murder of two fellow passengers.

The murders appear to be linked to a century-old legend involving a cache of gold stolen from a prospector and buried by two thieves.

Their seven-day cruise is spent hunting for the gold and eluding the modern day thieves intent on possessing it at any cost.

Another nail-biting mystery that will have you on the edge of your seat one minute and laughing out loud the next.

http://booksbybob.com/lady-justice-and-the-cruise-ship-murders_373.html

LADY JUSTICE
AND THE
CLASS REUNION

For most people, a 50th class reunion is a time to party and renew old acquaintances, but Walt Williams isn't an ordinary guy --- he's a cop, and trouble seems to follow him everywhere he goes.

The Mexican drug cartel is recruiting young Latino girls as drug mules and the Kansas City Police have hit a brick wall until Walt is given a lead by an old classmate.

Even then, it takes three unlikely heroes from the Whispering Hills Retirement Village to help Walt and Ox end the cartel's reign of terror.

Join Walt in a class reunion filled with mystery, intrigue, jealousy and a belly-full of laughs!
http://booksbybob.com/lady-justice-and-the-class-reunion_387.html

LADY JUSTICE AND THE ASSASSIN

Two radical groups have joined together for a common purpose --- to kill the President of the United States, and they're looking for the perfect person to do the job.

Not a cold-blooded killer or a vicious assassin, but a model citizen, far removed from the watchful eyes of Homeland Security.

When the president comes to Kansas City, the unlikely trio of Walt, Willie and Louie the Lip find themselves knee-deep in the planned assassination.

Join our heroes for another suspenseful mystery and lots of laughs!

http://booksbybob.com/lady-justice-and-the-assassin_395.html

WOLVES IN SHEEP'S CLOTHING

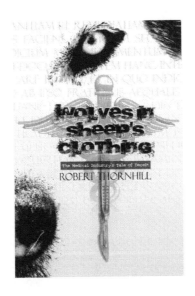

In August of 2011, I completed the fifth novel in the *Lady Justice* mystery/comedy series, *Lady Justice And The Sting*.

As I always do, I sent copies of the completed manuscript to several friends and acquaintances for their feedback and comments before sending the manuscript to the publisher.

Since the plot involved a holistic physician, I sent a copy to Dr. Edward Pearson in Florida.

Dr. Pearson loved the premise of the book and the style of writing, particularly as it related to alternative healthcare, natural products and Walt's transformation into a healthier lifestyle.

In subsequent conversations, Dr. Pearson shared that he had been looking for a book that he could share with his patients, colleagues and peers that would spread his message in a format that would capture their imagination and their hearts.

The Sting was very close to what he had been looking for and he made the suggestion that maybe we could work together to produce just the right book.

As I reflected on this idea, I realized that Walt's skirmishes with pharmaceutical companies, corrupt politicians, doctors, nurses, hospitals, bodily afflictions and a healthier lifestyle were not confined to just *The Sting*, but were scattered throughout all six of the *Lady Justice* mystery/comedy novels.

Using *The Sting* as the basis of the new book, I went through the manuscripts of the other five *Lady Justice* novels and pulled out chapters and vignettes that fleshed out the story of Walt's medical adventures.

Thus, *Wolves In Sheep's Clothing* was born.

Dr. Pearson is currently using *Wolves* in conjunction with his New Medicine Foundation to help spread the word about healthcare alternatives.

New Medicine Foundation
Dr. Edward W. Pearson, MD, ABIHM
http://newmedicinefoundation.com

RAINBOW ROAD
CHAPTER BOOKS FOR CHILDREN
AGES 5 – 10

Super Secrets of Rainbow Road

Super Powers of Rainbow Road

Hawaiian Rainbows

Patriotic Rainbows

Sports Heroes of Rainbow Road

Ghosts and Goblins of Rainbow Road

Christmas Crooks of Rainbow Road

For more information, go to
http://BooksByBob.com